GRAVE MAGIC

THE ACCIDENTAL REAPER PARANORMAL URBAN FANTASY SERIES

MISTY EVANS

Beach Path Publishing LLC

ONE

Suffocating fog slid heavy as a blanket over Shepherd's Rest. The historic Danté's Grove cemetery looked like a horror film set, the nearby mature oaks and straight-trunked pines blurry in the thick mist, assorted graves decorated for Halloween amongst the moss-covered headstones and weeping angels.

Scattered twigs cracked under my boots as I diverted from the disintegrating hundred-year-old path to stroll over the uneven ground. Ghost, my psychopomp, sniffed the base of a gravestone, and the echo of my raven's croak filtered down to me from the air. Corvus was trying to find our quarry from overhead, but it seemed he wasn't having any luck.

My own success was as thin as the toy skeletons caught on the nearest hedgerow. My witchy friend, Aurora, had done a locating spell for me and claimed the noncompliant soul I needed to reap was here. I'd searched every corner and crevice, every above ground crypt and mausoleum and found nada. Since this was Louisiana and most folks were buried above ground, it had taken an eternity.

No pun intended.

Not to mention I'd had to avoid two ghost-tour groups, along with a few ghost hunters who were filming snippets for their web shows and social media followers. Business was hopping for those who specialized in such things, as well as the local shops capitalizing on the season and the town's growing reputation for paranormal activity.

Not that Danté's Grove wasn't a hive for it; it was. The local humans had no clue they lived in a hotspot for supernaturals, though. The Chamber and town council wanted to spin our quiet community as a mini-version of New Orleans, and from all accounts, their campaign was working. Even my mundane friends had recently mentioned their unease about the recent spikes in murders and other crimes, each one having a mysterious, evil element to them.

Little did they know magic was real and there were many, *many* evil things coming to town.

Nicknamed Hell's Rejects, Danté's Grove boasted approximately twenty-thousand people, mundanes and magicals mixed together. The hardcore supernaturals lived off the grid, yet moved in the shadows. Competing with New Orleans was laughable, but we had our fair share of actual magic users, along with those who wanted to profit off the idea of it.

The pea-soup of this particular burial ground clouded my vision and weighted my limbs, making me feel eighty instead of twenty-five. My foot barely missed the corner of a raised piece of concrete denoting the remains of a couple who'd died decades ago. I felt a tremor of their spirits at my nearness.

Not tonight, I told them. No raising the dead on this mission. Necromancer and grim, I was nearing the end of my contract with Soul Management Group and only had one noncompliant left to harvest.

"Oh, *Trinity*," I sing-songed, bored out of my mind and eager to get home and ravish my partner, master vampire Killion Reveux. Just the thought of him made my toes curl in my boots. "Come out, come out, wherever you are."

While my scythe did not heat in my palm, nor did my official SMG skull and bones tattoo warm on my chest, I knew she was near from the faintest bit of residual magic floating on the mist. Having been a reaper for nearly a year—the term of my employment agreement with SMG —I'd learned my initial incarnation had been as Grim Zero back when the world began. Now I was simply Chloe Frost, Grim 281, 1st Class, but the original reaper was as much a part of me as my freckles and love for ice cream.

For months after I'd discovered the truth, Grim Zero had felt separate from me. Now we were as close as twins. The more I accepted and integrated her into my life, the more magic I possessed, including grave sight.

That special ability was why I could see the residual magic Trinity was leaving behind. Every supernatural had a magical fingerprint, and I could sense, smell, or see the lingering aftereffects of spells, hexes, incantations, and rituals. There was a lot in this ancient cemetery. Too much, in fact. Trinity was a dark magic user and an extremely powerful witch who was as old as this place. To say she was overdue on her life contract expiration date was a definite understatement.

I casually swung my scythe back and forth in front of me as I walked, cutting through the dense haze. Her residuals acted as breadcrumbs, leading me on, while my companions tried to help. "Trust me," I told the five-pound menace now sniffing at another grave marker, "she's not in the ground. Not yet, anyway."

Ghost raised her head, her long hair flat with the dampness, and gave a sharp bark.

"Don't get testy with me. If you'd eaten dinner before we left instead of napping in Killion's lap, you wouldn't be starving right now, spoiled dog." Normally, I brought snacks, since reaper work burned a ton of calories and the two of us were always hungry. Tonight, I'd been distracted by the sexy master vampire who'd been sipping from a goblet of expensive merlot in front of his fireplace, reading to me from his favorite volume of philosophy, and looking good enough to jump. The philosophy read like a long love poem in many ways, and I was surprised at that choice since he wasn't one for sentimentality. He'd been dividing his attention between my dog in his lap and the book, his deep voice flowing over me as I dressed in my black suit and boots before heading out on this job. I could still hear the purr of his voice in my head.

Chloe?

Oh wait. That actually was him. "Yes, my love?"

How long before you finish?

Being partners and soulmates was the reason for our telepathy. *Not soon enough.* "I thought she'd be easier to find," I groused and zeroed in on a cluster of her pulsing magic. As soon as I cut through it with the blade, it vanished, only for another to blink to life ahead. "She's eluding me. If I didn't know better, I'd think this fog was one of her spells. It glitters with her magic, but I can't seem to actually pinpoint where she is."

Perhaps that is how she has escaped her death for so long.

Probably. The witch traveled constantly, disappearing from the world in one spot, only to reappear in another decades later. I wasn't the first grim to be sent after her, but it was the first time she'd surfaced in this area of the southern United States. *She won't get away,* I told him. *Not from me.*

I stopped walking and closed my eyes, sending out a pulse of my magic to the far corners of the two-acre place. It was a last measure and a tricky one at that. The dead in their crypts were already aware of my presence, but the magic tickled at them and they began to draw on it, trying to plug into my necromancy and use it to recall their souls into their bodies.

Gently but firmly I blocked them, knocking their hands away from my life-giving cookie jar. Raising the dead to help me capture Trinity was out of the question, but I had other ways of sussing her out. My control over the level of magic had to be precise, though, so I didn't accidentally have zombies to deal with on top of her.

As my magic curled like a wave in slow motion against the perimeter of the stone fence and hedgerows, it echoed back. I closed my eyes and waited for my version of sonar to reveal where she was hiding.

A ripple rolled over me, feathering against my skin and alerting me to a living body. Behind my closed lids, Trinity's aura flickered and her heart beat, once, twice, three times. A beacon. *There you are.*

Killion: *This new portfolio is giving me a headache. Shall I come join the hunt?*

The mundane world knew him as a financial advisor and he did indeed have an incredible track record of making clients rich. In the supernatural world, he was a three-hundred-year-old Romanian hybrid—half vampire, half human—as well as my sworn *incatusa sufletum.* When called upon, he works as a detective for SMG. Together we investigate crimes against the dead and the living.

Our magical binding of souls was the rarest kind of love that existed. We shared everything and would be together forever, in this life and the next. It went beyond what humans termed soulmates, but the idea was the same—no matter who or what tried to part us, we would always have our bond to keep us connected.

Although he didn't need to sleep, I did. I had an important college final to complete the next day for one of the few classes left before I could take my state boards and become a full-fledged veterinarian. I also had to work at the clinic I owned. "She's on my radar," I told him, heading in the direction of Trinity's heartbeat, skirting around an angel statue. The witch had dampened the steady beat of her heart, but not enough that I couldn't tune in to it. When the dead under my feet reached out again, trying to snag me, I coiled my magic back in. *Sleep*, I told them. To Killion, I murmured, "I'll wrap this up and be home before you know it."

I'll be waiting.

The seductive tone of his voice sent a pleasurable shiver through me. The fact he didn't insist on rushing to my side to help, knowing how important harvesting Trinity was, also made me happy. Thanks to our bond, we'd gone round and round about his territorial need to constantly be at my side, ready to defend and protect me at every turn. While noble and romantic, being who I was —*what* I was—made me nearly as invincible as the master vampire himself. Problem was, I'd given away a lot of the years of my own life contract in order for other people to have extended years. I was down to less than five now. Our time was growing shorter by the day.

Definitely time to end this and get back to him.

The throb of Trinity's beating heart slid away as she vacated her hiding place.

"Stop running," I commanded into the gloom. "We both know how this is going to end. You stole several decades you weren't meant to have. Be grateful for those."

Noncompliant souls are a messy bunch. Stubborn, too. That's why Death, my boss, sends me after them. Not only because I am the original reaper and never fail, but because I tend to drive him crazy, and he likes to get back at me.

I tapped Ghost on the head and gave her the wordless hand signal we'd worked on. The Papillon-mix with ears the size of satellite dishes shifted into her monstrous psychopomp form, eyes lit with an internal glee. I'd never seen a true hellhound, but I suspected she was about as close to it as you could get in appearance. Drool dripped from her panting mouth, her body tense and ready to leap for the soul we were about to harvest.

The witch threw a spell at us. Instinctively, I sliced through it, but the reverberation made me gasp at the strength of her power.

I knew a thing or two about witches, having a close friend as one. Aurora had been around as long as Trinity, maybe longer, although she looked my age. She'd taught me a great deal about magic, and helped me harness my own abilities. Grim Zero had never needed to recite a rhyming incantation, or even think about how to channel her power—it had been as natural to her as breathing. For me, not so much.

I'd been reluctant to tap into the vast ocean of her magic, because it was too overwhelming. Killion had helped me considerably with my confidence about what I could do and how to control it. Along with Aurora, he'd been the catalyst for me accepting the extent of my necromancy. I no longer feared it, and gaining that knowledge had changed everything.

"Enough," I ordered. "You will not win this fight."

The fog around Ghost and I cleared, revealing a slight figure in black robes. The edges of her image seemed to fade and blend with the mist. As I'd suspected, the unnatural fog was her creation. "Correction," she purred, although her lips didn't seem to move. "*You* will not win this fight."

I preferred to be kind and gentle with those I was

harvesting, easing them into death and the afterlife. Noncompliants like Trinity didn't deserve kindness, and I knew my good intentions would be wasted. I extended the scythe. "Touch the blade. I'm tired, and I have a very sexy vampire waiting for me." Ghost whined. I cocked my chin at her. "Also, I need to feed my dog."

The psychopomp gave a fierce bark of agreement.

Trinity's black lips curved upward. I thought she was going to speak, but her hands emerged from the sleeves of her robe and she threw a glowing ball at me.

Instinctively I raised the blade once more, again slicing the spell in half. The midnight black energy disintegrated into a dozen glittering crystals that tinkled when they hit the ground. "Don't be rude," I growled.

And then I lunged.

She was fast, but not as quick as me. The metal of my scythe missed her chest by a fraction, but took off a section of fabric from the arm she threw up in defense.

Another spell blasted from her hand and I ducked and whirled from its path, slicing at her once more with my weapon. She dodged and laughed. "Queen of the Dead, you may be the incarnation of Hecate and the Morrigan, but my master will protect me from your blade, no matter."

My attention snagged on the term *master*. I halted my attack. "Who do you serve?"

She took a step backward, as if she would bleed into the night and disappear. "He sent me to find you. To test you. To start a war that even you can't stop."

"Yeah, well, there's been quite a few who've tried that and more. All of them have failed."

Her smile was confident. "We will not. *I* will not."

"Hello?" An unknown voice carried across the cemetery. It was indistinct and could have been male or female. "I search for the reaper."

Trinity bent forward, giving me a mock bow. "*Hir yw'r dydd a hir yw'r nos, a hir yw aros Arawn.* Until we meet again."

As the stranger rushed across the ground toward me, Trinity twirled her robes and vanished.

TWO

The fog vanished with her.

Orange and black flowers, pumpkins, and other fall decor were left bedraggled and damp from the remnants of Trinity's magic. The lawn was slick with it.

The stranger closing in on me had to be on his way to a costume party dressed as Alice Cooper. He was tall, angular, and had long, dark hair that practically glowed with beauty magic. The chains on his black boots jingled as he strode forward, and his matching leather jacket and pants sported enough hardware to sink a ship.

Baleful eyes, ringed with thick liner, stared out under his hat. Ghost cocked her head and shifted to shield me. She growled menacingly, causing him to stop and raise both hands. "Hey, love," he said, his voice soft, almost feminine. "I need your help."

I hid my scythe behind my psychopomp, letting it rest next to my leg. "The ghost tours are over until tomorrow night. They meet by the first mausoleum inside the gate."

Speaking of ghosts, several appeared close by, inspecting the newcomer. "I don't need a tour." He fell to his knees and clasped his hands in front of him. "You're the reaper, aren't you? I need you to kill me."

This night is full of surprises. "Sorry, you have the wrong gal."

I started to walk away, folding down and sheathing my compact blade in the leather holder strapped to my back. Mundanes could see it but believed it was a fake, especially this time of year when three-fourths of Dante's Grove ran around dressed in ridiculous outfits, consuming too much alcohol and Halloween candy.

Supernaturals recognized the weapon, as well my reaper robes, for what they were and the smart ones stayed out of my way. Killion's seamstress had modified the robes into my jumpsuit. No more tripping over the long material or getting the sleeves caught on my blade. I called it my Catwoman suit, and I had to admit, it was sexy as hell.

"Wait!" Alice Cooper jumped to his feet, but Ghost blocked him from following me. "You're a grim. *The* grim. I need you to take my soul before she does."

Pausing, I knew it was a bad idea to engage him. Unfortunately, as my friends can attest, curiosity often trumped my common sense. Longing to get out of the creepy cemetery and go home to a hot bath and a big meal—not to mention the master vampire waiting for me —I heaved a heavy sigh and faced the stranger. "Before who does?"

Corvus landed on the nearby iron gate, dancing between two of the fleur-de-lis topped posts. Our visitor barely glanced at the raven. "The malefactor you pursue. She and her wicked coven are using me as a weapon in their plans. You must take my life before it's too late."

He was a supernatural, but I couldn't put my finger on what kind. His magic was feathery and skirted away every time I tried to get a handle on it. "Cryptic pronouncements aside, I can't. You know how this works, right? I can only harvest souls that are on my list. Those whose life contracts have expired."

"Or anyone who threatens you."

Corvus squawked a warning. "Bring Aurora," I told him under my breath and the raven slapped his wings and took off. I opened my telepathy once more to Killion. *Listen.*

The male didn't appear particularly threatening, but I wasn't about to let down my guard. "It's not in your best interest to try anything." Now that the fog had cleared, it was harder to see the sparkling residual energy of Trinity's dark magic, but I could sense it in his aura. It felt razor sharp and prickly as a cactus. "If you want to help me harvest *her*, however, I won't turn down the offer."

His laugh was full of scorn and the prickly magic bristled. "Reaping her is impossible. Taking me out of the equation, however, will weaken her and thwart her plans. Temporarily, anyway, until she can capture another creature with divine magic. What is it about this you don't understand?"

The earthbound souls floating nearby watched with interest and I wanted to sick them on him. "My job is to take care of her. Until you're on my list, or you pose a viable threat, the rules are the rules." My boss, Death, would laugh hearing me say that.

"I heard you were known to break them when it suited you."

I looked him over from his hat to his boots, still unable to assess what kind of supernatural he was. There were layers and layers of spells and reflective magic coating him. At least one, if not all, set my teeth on edge, but determining his particular brand of magic was like sticking my hand on a cactus. Each time I tried to wiggle past it, I got a poke. "I can't take your life. Tell me why Trinity is using you, and what exactly she's planning."

He glanced left, then right. "Eyes and ears are every-where. It would be wise to find a safer location for a discussion of such things."

"The ghosts?" I snarled at the closest one and he vanished in a panic. The rest followed. "They're gone. They wouldn't rat you out, anyway."

"Trinity can speak to the dead as easily as you, and she has her ways. Horrible ways."

Meaning torture? I glanced about with my grave sight, checking for any more intruders and eavesdroppers. I saw none of the living. My magic sensed the dead, along with a few teenagers loitering outside the gate and daring each other to spend the night inside one of the mausoleums. Stupid kids. "Who are you?"

"Friends call me Gard, although, I don't really have any. I'm the channel Trinity uses to connect with her master." His black-ringed eyes darted around the space again and I saw his Adam's apple bob. He worried his hands, spinning a thick snake ring around his left middle finger. "She has trapped an angel and forced him into servitude. I'm the channel for it." His voice lowered to a whisper. "I dare not even speak his name for fear he will waken from his slumber. Once she and her coven achieve full control over him, their power will significantly increase."

"I assume she wants a power boost in order to enslave humans? Take over the world? Cheat death?" I'd faced my fair share of supes trying to do all of those and more.

"To wipe out all of you—vampires, werewolves, grims. All the beings that fall in-between. She will raise witches and wizards from the bottom rungs of the magic world to the top."

Why is she using him as this channel? Killion asked in my head. He'd been quiet, but I'd known he was taking all of it in.

I repeated the question aloud to my new friend. "Why you? How is it you can connect to this angel?"

Disbelief morphed his features, as if I were purposely being dense. "I am unique. I have gifts. Skills."

He said it with a side of *duh*, which he'd probably never actually said in his entire life. "Which are?"

Again, he seemed affronted that I didn't know. He held up the hand with the ugly ring, wiggling it at me. "I am the original keeper of the *Key of Holumdra*."

Whatever *that* was. "I appreciate the warning, but trust me, if Trinity is on my list, her days are numbered. You'll be free of her soon. Now, unless you can tell me her location, I'm calling it a day."

Corvus turned with a loud shout, "Kill!"

It was one of the few words he knew, and his favorite. Still, I wondered if Death had intercepted him and sent him back as a directive to follow through with Gard's request.

"Your familiar?" Gard asked. "Ravens don't travel this far south."

Those in the wild didn't. "A pet." Not that it was any of his business.

My palm wasn't itching for the death blade, nor was my reaper tattoo activating. I took that to mean Corvus' outburst was not an order from my boss.

Gard's head swiveled to the side. Ghost's did as well, ears pricking as if catching the sound of movement. "Please," Gard said again. "End it for me now, and save yourself torture and pain. Keep those you care about safe."

Even with my enhanced hearing, I didn't pick up on anything besides the teens still goading each other. "Is she back?" I reached for the scythe handle.

"She's everywhere," he whispered, and then he vanished in a poof of smoke.

"Awesome." There was nothing I liked better than a dire and foreboding statement before the issuer of said statement disappeared. I left the scythe in its holder, seeing Aurora on the other side of the rear gate. "You got here fast."

Tonight she was rocking a sapphire blue skirt that fell below her knees and a ginger colored cloak. "I was leaving Andy's when Corvus summoned me. What's up? Any luck with Trinity?"

I shook my head. My car was parked a block from the

entrance. With Ghost back to normal size and Corvus flying overhead, we walked that way together. The teens had fallen quiet upon seeing my witchy friend, her red hair and fiery attitude evident in every step. Maybe they weren't stupid after all. "I encountered a guy who claims to be in servitude to her and has been forced to act as a channel for her and an angel. He mentioned the Key of something. Holo... Holum..."

"*Holumdra?*"

"Yeah, that's it. And Trinity said something to me in some weird language before she disappeared, but I have no idea what it meant." Both she and Gard sure knew how to make use of dramatic exits. "Any thoughts? I need to catch this gal and move her on her way. My SMG contract won't expire if I still have outstanding souls to reap."

She grabbed my arm to stop me. "You're sure he said *Key of Holumdra?*"

"Yep. Why?"

Her brow creased. "It's a mythical text. Some believe it was a bastardization of the *Key of Solomon,* which was for trapping and using demons and angels. Covens, other supernaturals, as well as mortals, have searched the world over for it."

"Sounds like our girl has it, or at least one of its keepers."

"Perhaps so." She seemed stunned. "I knew she was desperate for immortality, but I didn't realize she was powerful enough to trap and hold an angel."

"Sounds like she's not doing it on her own. He mentioned her coven is involved, too."

A slender brow arched under her bangs. "That makes sense, but still. Containing an angel? That's magic far beyond what most can accomplish."

At my convertible, I stashed my weapon in the backseat. Corvus hopped back there with it, but Ghost insisted on riding in Aurora's lap. "When I rid the world of her, that should break their control, right?"

"Not sure. Did Gard mention what her endgame is?"

"To wipe out vampires, werewolves, grims...you get the picture."

"Elevating witches and wizards to top dog."

She said it with a bit too much awe in her voice for my liking. "In my book, you already are." I drove down the road, the headlights doing little to cut through the gloom. "I have to stop her."

"Of course." She shook herself out of her musings. "The *Key of Solomon* is real, a text that gave humans the power to summon and control angels and demons. It's still around—the humans who used it aren't. That should tell you it's not to be messed with, especially by those with no innate magic to begin with. Doesn't matter how powerful the spells are, you have to be equally powerful to hold that type of entity and control it. You don't and you end up dead. The *Holumdra* was said to specifically work on the most powerful of otherworldly beings. Archangels, archdemons. You get the picture."

"Maybe I can use it on Death." I sensed her eye roll. I took the turn for her place at Evil Eye Burials, a cemetery that didn't show up on the maps the Chamber handed out to tourists. "I need to figure out where she's hiding and get this over with, then her angel trapping won't be an issue. Can you use one of your pendulums, or another location spell and see if you can find the angel?"

Her Irish lilt ratcheted up a notch. "She's good at moving about, isn't she? Don't worry, we'll find her. Come in and I'll make tea."

I managed to glance out my window so she didn't see my grimace. *Hard pass.* I rolled to a stop to let her out. "I have to call it a night. I have a big day tomorrow."

Aurora blinked at me, confused. "She's controlling an angel, Chloe. If he gets loose, or she does somehow manage to use that text to force him to her will, it will be chaos. A lot of supernaturals could die."

In my head, Killion came to my rescue. *There are precautions we can take. I've alerted SMG and they are devising a plan. Come home. There's nothing more to do tonight.*

"The world isn't ending yet." I relayed what Killion had said. "Warn Andy and have him spread the word to the shifter packs to be on alert. I'll find out what SMG wants us to do, okay?"

She looked disappointed. "I want to know everything, and how I can help, all right? Call me later?"

"As soon as I hear from my boss."

She bailed and Corvus joined Ghost in the front seat. I watched until she was safe behind her magically shielded graveyard, then turned for home.

THREE

"You better be ready," I announced to Killion as I entered his penthouse with Ghost and Corvus. I hung my scythe on the hook near the door and kicked off my boots. "After I eat, I'm going to ravish you."

The dog greeted him with kisses, then rushed to her spot near the fireplace where her food and water bowls were full. She helped herself and growled at Corvus who smacked her with his feathers so he could steal some kibble.

Killion, in his chair, arched a sexy brow at me as I sauntered over for a kiss. A curl of dark hair hung over his forehead, his violet eyes a shade darker in the flickering light of the hearth. His tie was loose, his dress shirt impeccable with the sleeves rolled to his elbows. In one hand was a brandy snifter and his caramel and old library scent mixed with the warm notes of the liquor as I tugged him to me with his tie and bent forward to bring my lips to his.

Combustion. At the touch of our mouths, everything inside me went into overdrive, his energy braiding with mine and making me consider climbing into his lap before I had my dinner. I began unzipping my suit and he stilled my fingers.

A female voice came from the dining room behind me. "You were right, Grave Girl." I turned to find Katarina at the long, rectangular table. The vampire enforcer had her jet black hair divided into two pigtails and her bangs were shorter than usual. The red lips, winged eyeliner, and leather top with a deep V neck that showed off her perfect assets were normal. She hovered over a plate full of food and used her fork to point at it. "This shrimp étouffée is to die for. The sauce..." Her lips pursed and her eyes rolled up. "Divine."

I stuttered, zipping up my own exposed assets. "What are you doing here?"

A perplexed look tightened her sculpted brows. "Are you purposely being obtuse?" She chewed a forkful and swallowed, lifting a glass of red wine. Or maybe it was blood. "I'm eating."

I glanced at Killion, who still hadn't moved or said anything. The amusement on his face, however, had shifted, his eyes darkening as his steady gaze roamed over my body, a promise in them.

Reluctantly leaving him, I exaggerated the swing of my hips ever so slightly to let him know I could hardly wait to make him fulfill it. I stopped by the head chair and placed a hand on the back. "You don't eat."

"Sure we do." She motioned at the figure across from

her. Harlow, Killion's second in command, nodded at me. "On occasion."

"Hello, Chloe," Harlow said in her smoky voice. She always sounded like a jazz singer with two shots of bourbon in her after a night on stage. Unlike Katarina, she wore no makeup, had a buzz cut, and her bronze skin glowed from the soft chandelier light. Her nearly silver eyes always weirded me out a bit and now they danced with lighthearted mirth.

So glad she was enjoying herself at my expense. "You're in my seat," I grumped at Katarina. "You're eating *my* dinner."

Pennyworth, Killion's butler and the best cook in Louisiana, bustled through the swinging door of the kitchen with a bowl in hand. He teased it under my nose before setting it on the table beside an empty plate. "I have an entire casserole dish just for you."

Good thing. "You're lucky," I told the smirking enforcer. She loved to rile me up, both on and off the training mat. As my sparring partner and fighting coach, she'd roughed me over more times than I cared to admit, but she'd also taught me much. I considered her a friend, even though I probably shouldn't have trusted her with anything more significant than my toothbrush. Loyal to Killion was all that mattered, and she was that. Still, I loved to give her grief any way I could. "Or my final act as a reaper would be to hand you over to Death."

As I settled into the chair, Pennyworth opened a cloth napkin and placed it in my lap. I thanked him and allowed him to serve me. The smell of my favorite dish and the feel of Killion coming up behind me calmed my irritation.

Katarina chuckled under her breath and made a show of continuing to eat, licking her lips and giving me a confident smile. "Any time you think you can take me, I'm happy to remind you that you can't."

Harlow ran an admiring gaze over my suit. "Out hunting?"

I helped myself to a dinner roll, taking my time to butter it as I flashed the knife blade at Katarina. "My last noncompliant is being particularly...well, noncompliant."

Killion placed a goblet of wine in front of me and took his seat at the head of the table. "After what I heard from you," he said, "I thought it prudent to inform my nest about Trinity's plans. Katarina and Harlow volunteered to discuss the matter in person."

So it hadn't been his idea. He'd been as eager as I was to enjoy our night together without further interference. I'd make this quick, then. I dug in to the étouffée, suppressing my moan at its deliciousness. I was thankful Pennyworth was a top-notch chef, due to my need to consume generous amounts of calories every day. "I'm going to take care of her."

"We don't doubt that," Killion said. "However, precaution never hurts."

The three of them stared as I finished off the heaping serving in a few bites and helped myself to another. "You guys don't need to worry. She's been difficult to hunt down, but she can't elude me forever."

They exchanged looks and Harlow toyed with her unused fork. "Your abilities aside, it's crucial we don't underestimate her and her coven. Do you believe they have an angel?"

I shrugged. "Not sure yet. Either way, all I have to do is reap her. End of story."

Katarina wiped her mouth and tossed down her napkin. "We can't let her disrupt Bite or Bark Night."

"Bite or what?" I asked around a mouthful.

Harlow seemed completely stymied at my ability to eat so much so fast, blinking at me as she explained. "The delegation has decided that in order to continue our efforts to keep the peace with the shifters, we are holding a special Samhain event. Andy already okayed it."

Along with Killion, Andy, Aurora's shifter boyfriend and honorary head alpha in the area, had put together a group of Undead and shifters to form a committee of sorts to carry out this new, if tentative, allegiance.

"It's going to be at St. Anne's," Katarina added. "Our version of Trick-or-Treat."

I glanced at Killion and drank some wine. "But the nest doesn't have any kids, outside of Mason, right?" I glanced at Harlow. "He's a bit old for that sort of thing, isn't he?"

Mason, her teenaged son, was a vampire-human hybrid like Killion. He worked at The Smoking Bean, the same coffee shop where I had up until July, and he was dating one of my vet clinic employees. His caramel lattes were the best, and I wasn't sorry I'd had two of them earlier.

She dipped her head. "The packs have quite a few offspring but this is a social event for adults as well as children."

Putting these two groups together was like playing with dynamite. Turf wars had existed between them as long as time immemorial. One wrong move on either side and the place would erupt in death and destruction. "You're sure this is a good idea?"

"The church has been declared a neutral zone by both parties," Katarina said. "No one will violate it. The delegation—as well as yours truly—will ensure that."

Only a fool would cross her. Not to mention Killion and Andy.

St. Anne's was a unique structure that existed on two different planes. At one time, it had been a normal Catholic Church, devoted to prayer, guilt, and saints, but some very dark magic had gone down there and now it hovered in and out of this dimension and another, invisible to most. Killion and his nest used it as a safe house and a covert location for interrogations and training. It was where Katarina regularly put me on my backside with far too much glee.

She seemed confident about its new designation as a safe zone, and I wanted this policy of Killion's to work. He'd spent hours schmoozing, delegating, and holding meetings to discuss concerns and issues on each side. The rift between species had gone on long enough and wasn't good for either of them.

The master vampire at the head of the table had superior intelligence, cunning, and a shrewdness that sometimes left me in awe. I saw all of that and more in his eyes when I glanced his way. There was a deeper layer to his plans. "I get it." I pointed my fork at him. "The enemy of my enemy is my friend, and all that. Creating a vampire-shifter alliance makes you stronger to fight beings like Trinity who want to turn you against the other."

A quirk of his lips and a nod. That subtle but intense power of his oozed from each and every pore on his handsome face. "She's not the only one who wishes to rid the world of us. Together we're stronger against our common foes."

Reapers keepers, he was sexy when he was being strategic. Fidgeting under his gaze, I ran a foot up his pant leg and let my mind send him images of what I planned to do to him as soon as our guests left.

Nothing changed in his outward appearance, but he pushed a few erotic images of his own back at me. Between him and the wine, I flushed and became even more eager to wrap this up.

The meeting didn't conclude, however, for another twenty minutes. I finished my dinner, listening to the three of them deliberate about all the ways they planned to ensure the party went off without a hitch, including their confidence that no witch or other non-welcome entity slipped in and caused turmoil. As always, Pennyworth and his impeccable timing had him delivering a slice of chocolate cake with a scoop of my favorite ice cream at the exact moment I finished the étouffée and wine. "Coffee?" he asked, whisking the dishes away.

"None for me." I pushed back and rose. "But I do need sleep and a bath. I'll eat this in there." I pointedly looked at our guests. "I have a big day tomorrow."

"*Rigggght.*" Katarina chuckled. "You don't have to lie, Grave Girl. We know why you're kicking us out."

I slipped behind Killion's chair and rested my hands on his shoulders. "Is it that obvious?" I blinked innocently and heard him chuckle in my head.

Harlow stood, hiding a smile. "Master." She offered a head bow and walked to the exit.

Katarina lingered, sitting more comfortably in my chair and acting like she might stay the night. "We need to discuss what *you're* doing at Bite or Bark," she said to me.

My friend, Nita, had invited me to a party she and her boyfriend, JR, were holding at his home. He was also a good friend and one of the vets at my clinic. No way I was letting them down. "Sorry, we have plans."

Killion tensed slightly under my hands. I'd mentioned the party to him and I'd assumed we were attending as a couple. Now, it looked as though he would be acting as playground monitor at the church.

"*I* have plans," I corrected. *I know you need to be at this event,* I told him. "Besides, having a grim present would put a damper on things, wouldn't it?"

A weak excuse to get out of going, yet nonetheless true.

Katarina mirrored my earlier innocent look. "I thought your contract with SMG was up this week. You won't be a grim anymore, right? No robes, no scythe, no magic." She sat forward, pursing her still-perfect red lips. "Or are you re-upping?"

No magic. The words felt like a hammer to my belly. I would be plain old Chloe again, even though I'd still have Grim Zero's soul. After the past year, that thought both elated and depressed me. Having magic had a cool factor of a thousand. A billion.

Plus, there was Ghost. I glanced over my shoulder at where she slept contentedly by the fire. There was no way I was giving her up, yet, she loved her job of taking souls to the other side. Even if I negotiated to keep her as a pet, would she be happy?

"That will be all, Katarina," Killion said in a bored tone. Even so, I didn't miss the underlying warning. "We'll discuss the party further tomorrow."

She averted her eyes, rose, and tucked in the chair. "Yes, Master."

I followed her to the door, noting her overly erect posture. She never liked being reprimanded, especially when it involved me.

A year ago, I'd been a starving college student who hadn't had a good night's sleep since my parents had died in a car accident. Between my work and school schedules, I'd lived on caffeine and sugar, wrestling with nightmares and oblivious to the supernatural world. The ring on my left hand symbolized how far I'd come—the master vampire and I were planning our wedding and I'd already had a life beyond anything I'd ever imagined. Which did not include continuing my grim duties. "You and Harlow have everything under control. I doubt there's much I can add to your security measures, but if you truly need me, I'll rearrange my schedule for that night."

She stopped, frowned as if stunned. It was good to throw her off balance once in a while. "You're not really going to quit SMG, are you?"

After living three hundred years, Killion found detective work to his liking. He said it kept his brain active and gave him something beyond leading the Undead to focus on. Together, we were a good team, and that was another reason I hated to give it up, but being at Death's beck and call, as well as the fact that the clock was ticking for both me and Killion, I didn't want to spend my last few years chasing down the Trinitys of the world. "You just want to make sure I keep coming back for torture—I mean, *training*."

That brought a smile to her lips. "I haven't enjoyed myself this much in decades. You're so fun to beat up."

She was teasing. Mostly. I was never quite sure where I stood with her—one minute she acted like my friend, the next as though she wanted to kill me. I patted her on the back and pointed at the door. "I'm glad my pain gives you purpose. Now leave."

She did, and I turned to discover Killion behind me, the promise of the coming night together shining in his eyes. "Your purpose right now is to come here and let me peel that suit off you."

Pennyworth rushed past with my cake and ice cream. "I'll run your bath and leave this on the ledge." He was back in a flash, thanks to his vampire speed, the sound of the water running in the background. "I added your favorite bath salts. Good night!"

The door closed softly behind him and I smiled. "Yes, Master," I mimicked, then jumped into his open arms and laughed when his fangs nipped my bottom lip as he carried me to my bath.

FOUR

The next day I was bleary-eyed and sluggish but happy. I made a big X on the calendar—only five days to go until my SMG days were over.

"You should have seen it," I said to Killion, recalling the previous night. While I'd failed to bring Trinity down, it hadn't been a total loss. We now knew what she was planning, and understanding my target was half the battle. "I sliced right through her spells. It was so cool."

"So you mentioned." He stood in front of a floor-length mirror in the walk-in closet, knotting his tie. It was a rich amethyst that matched his eyes and the purple stripe of my hair. "Another new skill to add to your magical inventory."

The words sounded innocuous, yet weren't. Typical Killion. Under the surface they vibrated with things left unsaid. "My magical inventory that will soon disappear."

"Are you sure you want to give it up?"

"Give up reaping? Absolutely." I brushed my hair into a high ponytail and secured it. He glanced at me from the corner of his eye, and I side-eyed him in return. "I'm going to speak to Mei, see what conditions may or may not exist when my employment is over. There's no way Grim Zero and her magic won't influence me. I may still be able to tap into it, even if I'm not a reaper. I also need to talk to her about Ghost. She's my dog and I'm not letting her go."

He finished his tie. "I received a message this morning from SMG regarding Trinity's plans to ignite a war between the Undead and the shifters. They've asked me to look into it and assist you on your assignment."

I grinned, raising my hand for an old-school high-five. "Partners again. One last time."

He took my wrist and drew me in for a kiss that ended with us breathing hard and me clinging to him. "In this lifetime and the next," he murmured against my ear, his breath tickling the sensitive skin of my neck.

Lucky me. I cleared my throat and tried to rein in my lascivious thoughts. "I'm meeting Aurora at her place at four. She'll have a location for us to start our hunt."

He kissed me again and turned to go. "Good luck today."

I'd been keeping the worry about my final exam pushed to the back of my mind, focusing on Trinity. I couldn't ignore it any longer. I had to face reality. "I'm going to be late."

"Moss will drive you. You'll be ten minutes early and will ace the exam."

"From your mouth to the Universe's ears." Relieved I could fit in a quick review in the backseat of the limo, I threw my arms around him to hug him goodbye. "Thank you. For everything."

After returning my embrace, he walked me to the door, making sure I had my backpack and the breakfast sandwich Pennyworth had fixed for me. He gave my hand a reassuring squeeze. "There's coffee waiting in the limo."

Ghost scratched at my legs and I bent to pet her. Corvus said, "Kill," which I took to mean *good luck* and gave the raven a thumbs up. "You two be ready to go when it's time, okay?"

She barked and the bird squawked. The butler appeared, beaming. "I'll make sure they are. You're a natural veterinarian, and I know, like the master said, you're going to ace this exam!"

Their confidence in me was reassuring. Truth was, I'd cut my teeth on taking care of animals. My parents had both been vets and started Frosty Paws. I missed them every single day. In reality, their car accident had killed me as well, but my inherent necromancy had brought me back. My more recent experience on the other side had evoked total peace, and I knew my parents were in that space, regardless of what folks termed it. It made living without them a little easier.

But only a little. I wished with all my heart they could be present today, supporting me, and guiding me in my final courses to fulfill this dream.

In the elevator, I tried to focus on believing that although I couldn't see their spirits, they knew what I was doing and were, indeed, watching over me.

"Morning, Grave Girl." Killion's driver, Moss, held

open the rear door of the car and handed me a caramel mocha latte. The tall cup looked diminutive in his giant hand. He could have easily played pro football in his human days, his massive chest straining the buttons of his shirt. "Ready to kick some butt?"

I accepted the cup with The Smoking Bean logo. A part of me missed working there. "As ready as I'll ever be."

He sped us through town to the university, my phone buzzing with texts from a dozen friends and family.

Mason: *That latte is my creation. Knew you'd need it. You can thank me later.*

Nita (my best friend since grade school who was a huge Divergent fangirl): *May the odds be ever in your favor.*

Uncle Morty: *You got this, kid.*

There was even one from Death: *May the forces of evil be nowhere near your path to success.*

Okay then. I sent each one a thumbs up and hurriedly scanned my notes.

Two hours later, I walked out of the conference room with three other students on the fast track like me, dazed and praying I'd passed. The online classes I'd taken over the summer, along with my guidance counselor's appeal to the school, had allowed me to complete most of the required course work so I could graduate in December. While this test had seemed deceptively easy, I worried that I'd screwed up at least one of the major essays. My companions seemed to be in the same state, mentioning how brutal the questions had been.

Moss and the limo were nowhere in sight.

Lawrence, one of the guys who'd been in the testing room with me, saw me scanning the parking lot. "Need a ride?"

"No," my boss answered, materializing out of nothingness. Lawrence and I jumped at the booming voice that made my bones quake. "Get lost."

When the six-seven scowling embodiment of death issues an order, only fools ignore it. Normally, he doesn't show himself to mundanes, but today apparently, he didn't care. Lawrence gave me a *sorry* glance and ran for his truck.

"Well?" Death asked.

"Well, what?" I countered.

His Australian accent was thick this morning. It tended to vary by mood, along with the color of his hair. "The employment agreement. Did you sign it?"

My brain was still filled with surgical procedures and medication details. "The what?"

His scowl turned impatient. "Your revised reaper contract. I sent it to you this morning."

"I have no idea what you're talking about, and FYI, I've been in there for two hours." I needed to get to the clinic, and I scanned the lot again. Moss had probably gone to the coffee shop or done some other vampire-y thing and lost track of time.

Digging in my backpack, I brought out my phone to text him but before I could hit *Send*, Death grabbed it from me. "Focus. You passed by the way, so get over that and sign that agreement, 'kay?"

"I did?" I couldn't keep the grin off my face. Then I frowned. "Wait, how do you know?"

He pointed at his broad chest. "Death, here. I know a lot more than you give me credit for."

"You didn't mess with the exam, did you?"

He acted offended, placing a hand over his heart and rearing back. "Would I do such a thing?"

I wouldn't put anything past him. *Revised reaper agreement.* As I replayed the words in my head, curiosity teased my exhausted brain. "SMG wants me to stay."

"No kidding, Jessica Fletcher."

I scanned his face, his blond hair flashing gold in the sun. "Has your old age caught up with you? That's not my name."

He pinched the bridge of his nose and suppressed an eye roll, but I saw it behind his closed lids before he opened them. "You're the one who's always throwing out pop-culture references. I thought for sure you'd get that one." At my blank look, he ground out, "Jessica Fletcher, the lead character in Murder, She Wrote."

"Oh!" Vera, my landlady, loved the reruns of that show. "Hey, that's actually pretty good for you. You've upped your game."

He pointed at my cell. "Can we get on with this?"

"They want to negotiate?"

"Mei Han does not negotiate."

That wasn't entirely true, but my heart sank. "This is only an extension."

He touched his nose. "Bingo."

"Why would I want that?"

His face fell, shock registering. "Why would you *not?*"

Oh, I don't know. Because of the grumpy being

standing in front of me who made life a daily challenge and didn't appreciate me? "You might try harder to get me to reenlist."

I grabbed for my phone, but he jerked it out of reach, scrolling and poking at the screen before he finally handed it over. "Use your finger and sign on the line. I'll have Tinker stop by the clinic with the oath book later."

SMG was both old-school and modern. They used technology but also required antiquated blood seals for pacts. "I'm done bleeding for this job." *Figuratively and literally.* I could be just as stubborn as Mei, and she knew it. "Find someone else to fill my position. The only thing I want is Ghost."

"She's a psychopomp. She goes with the job. You quit and she is reassigned."

My heart hit somewhere around my feet. We'd see about that. "Know any angels being used against their will by a noncompliant witch?"

That got him off the employment train. "I know what Killion reported, but no one has heard of any being trapped. Could be a fallen. They're harder to track."

"My source claims she's using one of your kind to power up her coven."

He held up a finger. "First of all, you know I'm one of a kind, so there is no other being like me. I'm not some basic angel. Secondly, harvest her soul and we won't have to worry about it, will we?"

No one could claim Death was humble. "The guy was adamant."

He hated it when I knew something he didn't. "Your source is blowing smoke up your robes."

Moss arrived at that moment and I hopped into the back, not waiting for him to open the door for me. The chauffeur hated it when I did that. "Clinic, pronto," I ordered. "Please."

"You got it." He nodded at me in the rearview. "Boss sends his congratulations."

"About the exam?"

He grinned and twisted, sending a bulky arm over the seat to offer his fist. "Said you only missed three. Kicking some grim butt today, you are. Your fresh latte is in the cup holder."

I made a fist and bumped his, then snatched up the drink. "I have work to do," I told Death through my open window. "At my normal, mundane, and very satisfying clinic job."

"Sign the contract, Frost," he demanded.

As we sped away, I stuck out my tongue.

FIVE

How did you know? I mentally asked Killion a block from the clinic.

I'd opened our telepathy line as soon as I was sure Death wasn't following. Because of my boss' bond with Grim Zero, he could eavesdrop on conversations, especially if I was in close proximity. I suspected he tried to listen in on conversations between Killion and I from great distances, but Aurora and I had managed to use a charm to scramble them beyond a certain range. Like a radio signal that was too far away, all he'd be able to do was pick up bits and pieces.

I have my ways, Killion replied with no small amount of swagger in his voice. *You did well.*

Death denies knowing anything about this angel Trinity has trapped. Could my source be wrong or purposely misleading me?

His pause was short but thoughtful. *The one misleading you could be Death himself.*

The clinic was busy and I was thankful for the extra

caffeine coursing through my system. Patty, my office manager, and Dr. O'Leary, my lead vet, asked about the exam, but they were knee-deep in clients and outside of me telling them I thought it had gone well, we didn't have time to chat.

Around noon, Nita stopped in and fell into synch with me as I cleaned and sterilized instruments in preparation for our upcoming surgeries. Also a veterinary student, and my former partner in crime at The Smoking Bean, she knew her way around clinical procedures as well as she knew how to pull shots of espresso. She looked out of place, though, in her plum colored jumpsuit, wedge heels, and side ponytail. I made a mental note to buy new scrubs—mine had been washed so many times they were more gray than mint green these days and the once-cute bananas dancing across the material resembled something more akin to dog puke.

"You're sure there were no trick questions?" She didn't wait for my response. "I hate essays. I'd rather cut off my big toe. Why do they always have them?"

"Not my favorite either." I handed her a tray and a pack of gauze pads to line up on the counter. "You'll do fine when you take yours. I'll help you prep."

"My real problem is the fact I don't have my internship hours yet." She straightened a set of clean towels and leaned a hip against the table. "Would it be weird for me to do them here?"

I'd known this was coming and had nearly offered her a spot earlier in the fall. As booked as we were, it would be great to have an extra pair of hands, but she was dating JR, my other doctor. "I'm not sure I can give you enough hours to start. We could use help, but the clinic is only so big and our current vets can't take on more. I'm running them into the ground as it is."

"Soon you'll be a full-fledged veterinarian yourself. You'll need a tech to take your place."

That was true. "I know you can handle working with me, but what about JR? What if you two have a fight or break up?"

Her perfect brows pinched. "You think I'd let that affect my work?"

"I'm more worried about our friendship."

She threw her arms around me, suffocating me in some brand of expensive perfume. "Never."

Because Killion was my main investor and we were making a profit—slim, but still in the black—he'd mentioned it would be prudent to open a second location or acquire a mobile unit. I liked both ideas, but it was a time management issue for me. At least until I could quit reaping.

Quit reaping. Once again, the thought made my gut twist, even as it also made my chest lighter. I could be free to devote myself to helping animals and enjoying the few precious years I had left to live. How could I give up Ghost, though?

When Nita released me, I squeezed her shoulder. "Ultimately, it's my decision and I'd love to have you intern with us. But I have to talk to JR and make sure he's onboard with this. He's one of the best vets around and we're lucky to have him." I suspected he'd open his own clinic at some point and become my competition rather than my second in charge. That thought made me sad. "To start, I can only give you Saturdays and Tuesday afternoons, but it will be a paid internship. What about The Bean? Can you rearrange your hours there?"

"I have to pay bills, don't I? Gotta keep that job, so I'll do what I have to." She hugged me again, even tighter this time. "I'm so excited! This is going to be the most fun we've ever had."

I felt buoyant, too, until she opened her tote bag and pulled out a stack of bridal magazines with at least a dozen bright orange sticky notes marking pages. "This is your homework tonight. Find a dress. I can come over and help you select one, if you want. I can't pick my maid of honor gown until we know what you'll be wearing and what colors you're going with."

My stomach twisted again. "These magazines are overwhelming."

"The ceremony is only two months away. You probably can't get any of these on such short notice, but if we can narrow down what style you like, we can hit The Bridal Barn and find a similar one for you."

A barn for wedding gowns. Sounded like hell to me. The place had as many versions as the magazines, but I got her point. Trouble was, I had no idea what I wanted—I was a scrubs, jeans, and comfortable tops gal. "I was thinking of doing something simple, like my mom did when she and Dad married."

Her face fell. "You mean hippie clothes?"

My parents were born after that fashion time period, but my mom had an eclectic collection of tiered skirts and fringed everything. She'd worn a lovely jewel-toned, beaded blouse and an ankle-length skirt when they'd tied the knot at the courthouse.

My dad had also been a bit more grunge than hippie preferring t-shirts and ripped cargo pants over slacks and dress shirts under his clinic clothes. I still had a few of his and Mom's things in a trunk at my apartment. Dad's smelled like the light eucalyptus aftershave he'd always used and Mom's jasmine perfume brought back sweet memories of when I was a girl watching her get ready for their date nights.

I fingered one bulky magazine, the publication falling open to a striking ballgown. "I love the idea of being a princess, but that's not me." I had several slinky outfits Killion had commissioned for me and I felt gorgeous in them, but with the plunging necklines and long leg slits, they were more nightclub than formal wedding attire. "And have you seen the prices?"

"You're marrying a millionaire. He can afford it. You should get two, in fact. One for the ceremony and a separate dress for the reception. That's what I'm going to do when I marry JR."

"Poor JR. He doesn't stand a chance." Killion was more in the billionaire lineup, but preferred folks didn't realize how wealthy he was. JR's family came from old money, but he, himself, never flaunted it either. "Thing is, I want to buy it myself."

"That's precious," she said, full of southern *bless your heart*. "You don't marry a man like Killion in a cotton skirt and flip-flops. You're tying the knot in a freakin' castle, Chloe! He'll be wearing a designer tux!"

He was taking me to his family home in Romania,

and flying in my closest friends and family. I couldn't wait to sleep under the stars in the mountains and see a real castle. "I know, I know. I'm just not a satin and lace kind of girl."

"It's one day." She patted my cheek. "You can do it. And you'll be glad you did. Trust me. The pictures will be amazing."

I sighed. "Come to my place at six and we'll go through the magazine. Nothing outlandish, though, okay?"

She squealed. "Simple, elegant, and sexy. Check, check, and check!"

After she left, I finished setting up the surgical unit and headed for the break room. My vampire godmother, a.k.a. Pennyworth, had left a bagel sandwich and chips in the fridge for me. I downed those, and feeling the crash from the morning's caffeine, pillowed my head with my arms for a fifteen minute sabbatical.

Before I could blink, I found myself in Shepherd's Rest. Fog once more hung like cobwebs on the trees and hedgerows. The low murmur of unified voices chanted in the distance. Curious, I followed the rise and fall of the sound, even though I couldn't make out the words.

Soon I saw a group of robed women stood in a ring around a raised gravesite with three crumbling head-stones. Holding their hands palms up, their chant became more intense. Their sleeves draped and fluttered in the breeze. The magic glittered in the air, charging it, and making my skin crawl. The language they spoke was foreign, but as I moved to get a clearer view, I stopped dead.

Trinity, her face half covered by her hood, her red lips moving under it as she led the chant, stood at the center of the circle.

All around me, the dead woke en masse, itching in their tombs to rise. The ground under my feet trembled and a pulse of my power flared, soothing them so they wouldn't.

The instant it hit Trinity's coven, her head snapped up, eyes locking on mine.

The texture of her magic fractured like glass around me, icy pain raking down my spine. For a long, breath-held moment, I felt frozen, her energy spearing me in a hundred places, my blood turning to that glittering glass and shredding my heart, my lungs, my organs.

Feeling her push into my mind, I recoiled, and in the next instant, gasped, as I somersaulted out of the dream and sat straight up in the plastic chair.

"You okay?" Patty turned from the counter where she was filling her favorite mug with coffee.

"Yeah," I answered on reflex. I shook out my arms, my hands tingling from lack of blood flow. "Guess I fell asleep."

"Can I get you something? You look awfully pale."

"Nah, I'll be all right in a minute. I didn't get much sleep last night, worrying about the test." I rose and stretched, the remnants of the nightmare sticky. The sensation of someone watching me hung like the burial ground's cobwebs. "Better get ready for the afternoon appointments."

She left, frowning, and I heard a knock at the rear

door. Aurora was on the step, also frowning, when I answered. "What did you just do?"

"Nothing...?"

She pushed her way in and glanced about, pulling me into the corner of the room where stacks of bagged pet food and two rows of kennels, a few with occupants, stood. "I felt a disturbance. It came from you."

"I had a dream. A nightmare. Something." An involuntary shudder wracked me when I recalled Trinity's dark, bottomless orbs. "I was in the cemetery and Trinity was there with her coven. They were doing a seance, I think. Stupid witches were about to raise the whole place."

One brow quirked. "They were raising the dead?"

"I could feel it."

"In a dream?"

I nodded, wiping at my arms as if I could remove the sticky magic clinging to me. "I stopped her."

"Did you, now?" The lines on her forehead deepened, along with her Irish accent. "You're sure about that?"

"It was just a dream."

"I don't think it was." She glanced toward the hall, checking to be sure no one was in hearing range. "You actually sent out a strong wave of necromantic magic. You've not done that before in your dreams, have you?"

I shrugged. "What else could it be?"

She grabbed my hand, exposing my wrist. Thin scratches shone white but didn't hurt. "Did she harm you?"

The memory of her magic raking my spine made me

tense. Had she actually done damage? I shook my head. "That's only a cat scratch." Except I hadn't worked with any that morning. "Her eyes were weird and her magic felt like knives."

"Lift your shirt."

"What?"

"Do it."

I relented and dragged the ratty hem up over my stomach. More pale scratches. "I'll be grimmed," I said. "How did that happen?"

"I was afraid of this," she said, shaking her head.

"Afraid of what?"

"It wasn't a dream, Chloe." She traced a scratch. "More like bilocation and she marked you, even though you weren't physically present, probably testing her powers."

"You mean, like astral travel?" I scoffed. "Right. How could I be in two places at the same time?"

She wasn't laughing. Not even smiling. "You can do a great many things we've yet to discover, and may I remind you that you've transported yourself through time and space previously without trying. You've been to Killion's castle and met his deceased parents. We've only seen the tip of the proverbial iceberg with your magic."

She was right—when I'd recovered Killion's family ring, I'd had a moment of psychometry. I'd traveled back in time and seen his mother when she was pregnant with him. His father, too. "You think I actually projected myself... Wait. If I did, then that means Trinity is there. Right now!" I grabbed her arm. "We need to get there. Fast."

"The two of us taking on Trinity with her whole coven backing her up?" She laughed, bitterly. "Without a plan, no less? No thanks. I don't have a death wish."

I was already calling Nita. "Hey," I said when she answered. "Any possibility you can double back and handle some checkups for me?"

"Right now?"

"Yes. You down for it?"

A pause. "Sure, I'll be there in ten."

"Perfect. I'll let Patty and Dr. O'Leary know."

As I disconnected, I gathered my backpack from my locker, calling to Patty that I had to run out for a few minutes. The Irish witch shook her head. "This is a bad idea."

"The best kind," I told her, shoving her out the door.

SIX

Gunmetal gray clouds gathered over the cemetery's old, abandoned, and dilapidated church to the east.

"Do you see that?" I asked Aurora.

"That ugly corona over the building remains? How could I miss it?" She drew a pendant from under her shirt and murmured a quiet spell of protection. "Whatever Trinity and her coven are up to, they're also brewing up a storm."

She parked and we got out, me drawing my scythe. Aurora said another spell and flicked her fingers at the air over our heads. Bursts of sparkling magic formed a barrier around us.

"You should have seen my blade slice through the spell she threw at me last night," I told her as we trudged toward the entrance. "It was way cool."

"Your powers have grown immensely." she scanned the tall posts of the double-gated entrance, stopping me before we crossed the opening. "Let me check something."

I stepped back, twirling the scythe handle in my palm. No heat there or with my tattoo. Hmm. "Why doesn't Trinity's boy toy off himself if he wants to stop her?" It was something I'd thought about last night when I couldn't sleep.

Her fingers traced an invisible line in the air. "She may have a hex on him so he can't."

Made sense. "There's something not right about him, and it's not because of his connection to her. I don't trust him. How is it he's out running around free if she's controlling him?"

Her fingers sparked again, this time sending a blue-coated light over the gates. A sigil flared bright above us and winked out, burned away by her magic. "There," she said, brushing her hands together. "We should be fine now, but keep your wits about you. If there's one, there's more."

Tentatively, I stepped across the threshold into the graveyard. "What was that thing?"

"It acts as a tripwire to let her know we're here."

I peered over my shoulder toward the dilapidated church. "Is it possible she moved outside the graveyard to do whatever she's up to?"

"We can check that out after we see what she's up to. The dead seem quiet."

They did. No spirits lingered and those buried did not awaken as the two of us moved cautiously along the path. It was a relief, but it might also mean Trinity had already done what she came to do. "I can't figure her out.

Both of them vanished in a puff of smoke, like a stage magician."

"Interesting, but don't underestimate her because of a parlor trick." She glanced toward the church. "This may be a job that requires more than us. I think you should call for backup."

"Already did."

She nodded approval. "Now, where did you see them? This place is two acres of dead folks I don't care to stumble about over, especially if Trinity and her coven are raising a few of them."

A breeze blew past us, tangling my hair. I dragged a strand off my cheek and tucked it behind my ear. "They were on the far edge to the north," I pointed. "There was a row of gnarled trees behind them. Not far from where I encountered her last night."

We headed that direction, eyes and ears alert. My magic tingled as we drew closer, but there was no fog, no sparkling chips of black magic leading the way. I stopped for a moment, pivoting slowly in a circle to scan the markers as far as I could see. I sent out a subtle pulse, waiting for my sonar to bounce back.

"I saw the bridal magazines on the table," Aurora said. "Still haven't picked a dress?"

"Nita and I are going to look through them tonight. Hopefully, I'll be inspired."

It wasn't really an answer, and yet it was. Aurora knew me as well as Nita did. Just in different ways. "Are you getting cold feet?"

"Don't be ridiculous. You know better than that. I simply can't see myself in a traditional gown."

She chuckled. "It does seem a bit out of place for you, especially with you marrying a vampire in a spooky old castle. Yards of tulle and white lace seem…"

"Like a horror movie waiting to happen?" I nodded. "When I was a kid, I thought I wanted a big, showy wedding, but now that I can have one, it feels… Weird." I glanced her way and saw her patient smile. "Maybe it's because my parents won't be there. Uncle Morty's doing the honors walking me down the aisle, but…" My throat constricted.

"You always thought your dad would. I get it."

I fiddled with the handle of the blade. "I've found myself rethinking everything, you know?"

A nod. "A traditional ceremony doesn't quite fit a master vampire and a grim reaper. Maybe you need to think outside the coffin."

"Ha ha." This was an opening I couldn't pass up. "Have you ever considered marriage?"

Andy had asked her more than once; she'd always turned him down. "I can't and won't be chained to another."

"Is that how you see it?"

The corners of her lips slid down. "It's an archaic system meant to control women. I'll have none of it."

"Killion is my mate for eternity and has no desire, nor reason, to control me."

"Yes, so you believe."

"Aurora!"

Her hand waved me off. "Sorry, I'm not in the best of moods today. You're bound to him and thrilled about it. If you want to take vows, it's none of my business."

"I thought you were happy for me. For us."

"Of course I am."

She didn't sound like it. The subtle pulse of my magic rebounded back to me with no indication of Trinity or anyone else—with the exception of the dead, of course. I shifted gears, deciding the conversation needed a pin stuck in it for now. "She's gone."

Aurora took out a small crystal ball and held it in her palm. Inside, a tiny cloud of smoke twisted and curled. "She's here somewhere."

"Because your ball says so?"

One eyebrow quirked at my tone of doubt. "The smoke settles if it can't detect her."

From the way it was moving, she had to be close. "I'm telling you, the only entities inside the gates are you, me, three squirrels, a bunch of birds, and two-hundred and sixty-three dead folks. One recently buried." I waved a hand under my nose. His spirit was fresh—so was the embalming fluid in his veins.

"You can smell him?"

"Unfortunately, yes. My magic tells me far more than I need to know about folks in places like this."

"How curious."

"Like my astral travel? Can't say I enjoyed that. Neither do I want a repeat encounter with Killion's father. Luckily, the family ring hasn't ever transported me back there."

"That was advanced magic, to be sure." She motioned at the headstones. "I still want to see who the gravesite belongs to, if you can find it."

I snapped off a fake salute. "Reaper bloodhound at

your service." I tried to pick up Trinity's residue, caught a tickle of it. The storm clouds over the church continued to churn in the distance. I searched for a safer topic than my upcoming ceremony. "I think I passed my final, by the way."

"Congratulations." She tucked the ball into her cape pocket. Her tone sounded resigned. "You'll be a veterinarian before you know it."

"It's all I've ever wanted—to help animals."

"So you're definitely giving up reaper work?"

I paused, tapping the blade against my leg. So much depended on it. "You sound disappointed."

She shrugged. "Magic suits you, and it's part of your life now, like it or not. It's been nice having you for a friend."

"We'll still be friends, Aurora. My grim status won't change that."

Her lips thinned and she glanced away.

Justifications tumbled through my head. "I want to live my final years my way, not at Death's beck and call."

"I understand."

Did she? We walked on, rounding a curve. A Virgin Mary on a pedestal extended open arms beside the entrance to a small mausoleum. "Magic is the bomb, don't get me wrong. I don't want to go back to being mundane, but what choice do I have? The clinic and Killion are my life. Being a reaper has consumed at least a thousand hours of my time in the past year. A thousand! Not to mention screwing up my sleep, bailing on the clinic, and a million other little things, like missing dinners with my aunt and uncle."

"You've added it up?"

"Being on-call 24/7 keeps me on edge all the time. Coming up with excuses to bug out and go harvest a noncompliant, like today with Nita, is a constant weight on my shoulders."

"Yet, you took the time to figure out how much it takes."

I slowed. "So?"

"You've given it serious thought, not turning in your robes."

"It's a tough decision. I'd love to keep my powers and I can't give up Ghost, but this"—I waved the blade around—"is exhausting and it takes me away from the clinic and Killion far too much."

"Hmm."

The tickle grew stronger and we arrived at the spot I'd seen during my astral visit. I read the grave markers out loud. "Maxwell and Tilly Gray." The third was an unnamed male child who'd died shortly after birth. "Ring any bells?"

She used her phone to snap a few pictures. "None, but I'll research them when I get home."

At least we weren't in danger of an attack from the coven. Both relieved and disappointed, I used my scythe to swipe through the lingering trace of obsidian residue. It was dull today. "You wouldn't happen to have a spell to grant magic to a mundane, would you?"

Her laughter was more bitter than her frown. "Afraid not. You're either born with it or acquire it through alchemy, like becoming Undead." The laughter died on her lips and her eyes widened. "You're not considering letting Killion change you, are you?"

"Become a vamp?" I screwed up my nose. "No way. I may love one of the Undead, but I never want to be one."

She laughed again, lighter, although strained. "Good." Another glance at the crystal ball and she pinched her lips. The smoke was still active, sliding against the edges and folding over and over. "She has to be here, but where?"

I held out the blade toward the clouds. "My Spidey sense says that way."

"Yes, mine, too. Best to wait for our backup, though. Whatever is brewing in those clouds is bad news. She's turned that church into a dark artifact. I can feel it."

Those were rare but dangerous. I had experience with a few types and their power sources tended to be the dead. "Is she collecting souls and holding them there? Like a prison?"

"Not sure. Can you sense any holy energy?"

I was only familiar with Death's version, but he *was* an angel of some sort. I reached out with my magic and tried to sense what was swirling around the sad structure. It was prickly and sharp, those cactus thorns once again. "Not a drop, but I can't really touch it. You?"

Her lips firmed. "No, but there are layers of vile and repugnant wards on it."

"You think that's where she's trapped the angel?"

"As far as I know, nothing can entirely conceal nor obscure angelic or demonic energies, so if this angel were in there, we'd know it."

"Could it be trapping Gard?"

"Like you said, he was running around, seemingly free. He doesn't appear trapped."

While I'd encountered a few dark artifacts, I was more familiar with fictional rather than real ones. I knew they were created with and held sinister energies. Few magic workers could handle them, even experienced witches.

A branch snapped behind us and I whirled, blade ready to strike.

Andy stepped from the trees, hands raised in supplication. "I come in peace."

"Did Killion call you?"

"No." He lowered his hands and scooped Aurora into his arms, causing her tinkling laugh to echo around me. "She did."

She kissed him and he held her by the back of the head, deepening it. I turned away and headed the way we'd come.

They caught up with me at the gate. A long, black limo sat behind Aurora's car. Moss waved from the driver's seat.

Ghost rushed at my legs and I lifted her, allowing her to get in a few enthusiastic kisses before I returned her to the ground. She ran off to pee near a tree.

Killion leaned against the side of the car, legs crossed at the ankles and that curling lock of hair falling across his forehead. I picked up my stride and he opened his arms as I drew close.

My turn for a hug and kiss. "Thanks for coming so quickly," I said against his lips.

A hand stroked my back, lingering at my hips. "My pleasure."

"So what do we have here?" Andy stood with Aurora on the dirt road leading to the church, tufts of grass and weeds growing in among the bare, rutted tracks. The shifter sniffed the air as tiny bolts of lightning flashed inside the clouds. "Smells dark, some kind of blood magic. There's an odd tinge to it."

"Like what?" Aurora asked.

He thought for a moment. "Sulfur?"

We exchanged a glance. Killion took my empty hand, twining his fingers with mine, and we joined them on the road. "Risky to perform in broad daylight," he said.

Aurora agreed. "She's good at trickery and spells, that's for sure, yet so far, I've seen nothing to suggest she's as powerful as claimed. A lot of showmanship, but nothing more than that. Unless, of course, she actually *has* snared an angel."

Silence hung between us as we turned that over. "Is this a trap or distraction?" I asked the group.

Killion scanned the area. "Both would be my guess."

At that moment, a bright light burst inside the clouds. I raised an arm to shield my eyes, as did Aurora. Andy instinctively shifted her behind him and Killion moved so fast, I hadn't realized he'd jumped in front of me until I blinked open my eyes. The clouds instantly disintegrated.

I peeked over his shoulder, eyeing the crumbling foundation and dilapidated walls of the church. I'd heard the ghost tour guides talk about it falling to ruin after a fire. "What the reapers was that?" Before any of them could respond, my eyes caught movement inside the cemetery walls. "There! That's her!"

My feet were running before I even finished. In her flowing cape, she ducked behind a copse of trees as I cleared the open gates. Ghost barked playfully, ready for the game, and Killion kept pace with me.

"Andy, get to the north entrance and cover it," he yelled. "Aurora stay here and guard this one."

My grim abilities, and the fact I now borrowed a few from Killion, included speed and grace. I was thankful for both, because plain old Chloe had neither. The master vampire was still faster, and shot me a cocky grin as he dashed past and jumped over a crypt on his way.

"Show off," I called, hopping over the same crypt and landing squarely on my feet. Like a snake, we serpentined between and over obstacles in our way, including giant grave markers and statues.

Over the next several minutes, we covered the entire two acres, but she was gone. Again.

"How does she do that?" I growled, frustrated.

Andy, in wolf form, leaped on top of a concrete mausoleum housing several family members. In a flash, he shifted to his normal self, sitting and dangling his feet over the edge. "I never saw her. She did not exit here."

Ghost sniffed around as we made our way back to the main entrance and Aurora. "Did you catch her?" the witch asked.

"Nope," Andy said. "There must be a secret underground tunnel or something she's using."

"I've surveyed the maps of this area," Killion told him. "No such tunnels exist in this section of town."

I ambled toward the church, Aurora's statement about Trinity being tricky. "There's no angel here, but maybe she wanted us to believe there was."

Aurora grabbed my arm, stopping me. "That may have been what the storm show was for—to get us to run willy nilly into an ambush."

"Or a cage," Andy added.

Or a bomb. While no one said it, I knew we were all thinking it. Earlier in the year, we'd been investigating the murders of several humans and a bomb had nearly killed us all.

My phone buzzed. I checked and saw I'd missed six texts from Nita and a call from Patty. "I've got to get to the clinic. What should we do?"

"I'll have Katarina inspect the foundation for magical trip wires," Killion said. "Let's meet back here at sundown and lay in wait for the coven."

"The ghost tours start then," I reminded him, "and won't be done until ten or later."

"Fine." He guided me to his limo. "We'll reconvene at midnight."

I nodded, frustration burning inside me. This was my job, and I was failing. "Bring your A-game," I said to the others. "I think we're going to need it."

SEVEN

The afternoon passed in a blur. Patty caught me between appointments to chastise me about hiring Nita without going through her.

"She hasn't even filled out the employment forms." She waggled a three ring binder at me. "She needs training on our system. You asked me to develop all of this, and yet you completely ignored it by hiring her on the spot."

"I'm sorry." I was, too. I wished I could explain and tell her it wouldn't happen again, because that's what she needed to hear. Unfortunately, I couldn't bring myself to say the words. This was the type of situation that came up frequently. It wasn't the first time I'd had to bail on her and our patients.

"I realize you have a lot going on," she continued, her tone a taut string, ready to snap, "but this is unacceptable. If you want me to be the office manager, you have to let me actually manage. You may have gotten away with winging it in school, but this is real life, Chloe. You owe this place and us respect. Our reputation and the responsibilities that entails is on your shoulders, but it's on mine as well."

Again, I wanted to reassure her that I was not irresponsible, but my actions proved otherwise. I couldn't exactly reveal that I'd been at a graveyard trying to stop World War III in the supernatural community. "You're right. I'll do better."

I hoped that was true.

Validating her feelings seemed to help. She lowered the binder. "Because Nita is your friend, and Dr. O'Leary gives her high marks as a student, I've waived the thirty-day probationary period. And she's coming in tomorrow to apply officially. I'll give her some hours next week. Okay?"

"Thank you. She's going to be a good addition to our team."

"I hope so. Workplace romances can be sticky."

"I'll keep a close eye on things. If she and JR have any issues, I'll be the one to step in and handle it."

"Good." She turned on her heel and went back to the reception desk.

I breathed a sigh of relief. She kept the place running and I needed her. I liked her, and the fact that she had known my parents meant a lot to me. It was nice to be able to talk to someone about them. Her friendship and support meant the world to me.

But honestly, I'd rather face down a rabid shifter than an upset office manager swinging a binder.

That afternoon, my landlord, Vera, brought in Petey, her parrot, for a checkup. When I went to get her from the waiting area, she was chatting with Fred, the janitor at the hospital. He and I became friends after I saved his life last year. His greyhound mix sat on the floor beside him, cocking his head at the bird as it picked up random words and repeated them.

"I love pets of all kinds," Vera was saying. She looked nice in an orange dress with pink flowers on it.

"Me, too." He petted the dog's head, his work pants covered in hair. "I've adopted three retired greyhounds in my life, but also had a passel of cats, a hedgehog, and a goat."

Vera's eyes widened. "Do you live on a farm?"

"I wish," he said. "I did as a kid. I'd love to have a place with a few acres someday. Had to give up my house a while ago, since I couldn't keep up with it due to my bad hip. Me and Ranger, here, have been in a rental for the past six years. Not a great place, to be honest, but they allow pets. My hip is better, but the housing market is so crazy right now, I can't afford a big place."

Patty handed me Petey's file and I motioned Vera toward the rear. "Sorry to break this up, but I have to keep everybody on time or the taskmaster back here"—I cocked a thumb at Patty—"will have my head."

Vera came to her feet, picking up the bird's cage and smiling at Fred. "It was nice to meet you. I hope you get that farm one of these days. If you do, give me a call. I'll help with the animals."

Fred stood and offered a hand. "Nice to meet you, too. I know it's forward of me, but maybe we could have coffee someday? I'd love to hear more about your sister's rescue. Maybe I could volunteer once in a while."

Vera turned three shades of pink and ran a hand down her dress. "Well, I think I'd like that. How about tomorrow morning at The Smoking Bean?"

"Ten?"

She couldn't hide her smile. "I'll be there."

In the exam room, I chuckled at her flustered expression. "He's a good guy," I told her. "And he's single."

Blushing harder, she waved me off. "Don't be trying to play matchmaker now."

Petey was the healthiest I'd ever seen him and I shared Vera's number with Fred after they left. I stayed late, catching up on paperwork and prepping for the following day. The busywork allowed the other part of my brain to turn over my situation with Trinity, SMG, and the things Aurora had said. The one box I could check was having that exam out of the way and knowing I had passed.

At the appointed time, I left and headed to my apartment to meet Nita. She brought street tacos and a bottle of tequila. Soon, we were mixing up margaritas down in Vera's kitchen.

"I love weddings," Vera said. The parrot was keeping us company, where bridal magazines were spread across the table, along with our food and drinks. "With your curves, Chloe, a mermaid silhouette would be striking."

She pointed to a model in an hourglass gown with beaded lace and a ruffled hem. It was beautiful and also constricting. Even with my newfound grace and balance, I'd end up on my face trying to walk in something like that.

Nita shook her head, flipping open a different magazine to one of her sticky notes. "Look at this strapless sheath. Modern, effortless, enchanting."

Perfect for *her*. "I like the sequins," I admitted around a mouth full of taco. The food truck she'd gotten them from had the best homemade salsa and I spooned more on mine.

"What's your favorite?" Vera asked.

I didn't have one. "There are too many to choose from. They're all beautiful, and the designs you two have picked out would definitely be in my top fifty."

"What about Killion?" My landlady finished off the last of her margarita and got up to get another. "What would he like to see you in?"

"This is not the 1950s," Nita scolded. "This is about what Chloe likes, not him."

"This from the woman who earlier said I was marrying a millionaire and he could pay for my gown," I reminded her.

She rolled her eyes.

Vera already had a flush from the alcohol and it turned redder. "I'm not suggesting he pick it. Chloe should get whatever she wants, of course, but it never hurts to know what the groom likes."

I had no doubts that Nita would want JR's opinions if they ever got this far, regardless of her feminist beliefs. "He'll like anything I show up in. I could wear a garbage bag and he'd be happy."

Nita nodded. "That's the best kind of groom. You really are lucky, Chloe."

After we finished our meal and enjoyed some of Vera's homemade cookies, I hugged my best friend goodbye and promised we would check out The Bridal Barn after Halloween.

Helping Vera clean up, I noticed she was frowning. "Are you okay? Is your heart bugging you?"

"My heart is fine. Doc says so. I've been feeling really good, actually. I just realized that you won't need your apartment after the wedding. Not that you're here much these days, anyway. I'll need to rent it out. That makes me sad."

My mind flashed to Fred. "Too bad you have a *no men* rule."

Dropping that little nugget caused her to pause and narrow her eyes at me. "Why do you say that?"

I played dumb, shrugging. "You might keep your options open."

"You're not suggesting what I think you are."

"Fred likes his coffee black, in case you were wondering."

"I certainly wasn't. I haven't thought anymore about him."

Sure she hadn't. "Between the two of us, we'll find a good match for you and the apartment. I promise."

I wouldn't leave Vera in a lurch and having a guy as handy as Fred around here would be good for her, but one way or another, I'd be sure I found the perfect replacement.

Perfect replacement. The words echoed on the fringe of my mind as I stacked the bridal magazines. An idea emerged and I wondered how to pull it off. I'd need help, but maybe...

Maybe I had at least *one* of my problems figured out.

She sent me on my way with cookies, and I smiled all the way to Killion's. It was only eight; we had hours before we had to be at the cemetery and I knew exactly how to fill the time.

That smile fell off my face when I found Death lounging in front of the fireplace with Killion. Each held a squat glass of brown liquid.

I hung my backpack and jacket on the hook near the door. "No, I haven't signed the employment agreement," I announced, perturbed, "and I'm not sure I'm going to. I have things to think about. My future to consider."

I turned to find both of them staring at me nonplussed. "What?" I asked and pointed to Death. "Isn't that why you're here?"

Begrudgingly, he rose to his feet, setting the glass on the coffee table. "Friends get together and have a drink once in a while." He glanced at Killion. "Thanks for the cognac. We'll talk again later."

He brushed past me and closed the door. I turned to the master vampire, still relaxing in his chair and staring into the flames. "What was that all about?"

"Trinity and her artifact."

Death had told the truth—it wasn't about me. "Did he have anything helpful to say?"

"SMG is dodging my questions regarding disclosure surrounding Gard and Trinity. I had asked him to pursue it, so he requested a copy of Trinity's soul contract, but was told it was unavailable."

"He's the one who handed down the order. How did he not have a copy? He always sees them."

"He claims Mei gave him the order and he passed it to you."

This obviously disturbed him. "What are you thinking?"

"Along with the fact that she claims there is no missing angel, I find it suspicious. Many creatures, including those labeled as divine beings, do not have soul contracts like you and I. They do not fall under SMG's authority, yet I know that the organization keeps tabs on them. Knows their whereabouts."

"So Gard's lying. Trinity doesn't have an angel yet." I shrugged. "And whether Death has seen her contract or not, we know she must be past her expiration date."

"Death said he wants to look into it further. What Gard is not, is a keeper of that text."

Another trick. "Is he even working with Trinity?"

"Probably, and we need to know more about him, yet SMG is once again unhelpful at the moment. It seems our witch isn't the only entity leading us on a merry goose chase."

"I've been thinking about that." I removed the drink from his hand and climbed into his lap. "It's time for us to set our own trap."

He eyed me. "Such as?"

"I'm calculating some odds and evaluating what our best move would be." I dipped my head to kiss his jawline, under his earlobe. "Guess I've been hanging around you too much."

His chuckle was low, sensuous. "Never."

We ended up in the bedroom as I'd anticipated. The feel of his body moving against mine blocked all thoughts of wedding gowns, noncompliant witches, and grim reaper contracts from my mind.

Later, on the drive to the cemetery, it all came rushing back.

Killion caressed my hand. We sat in the limo, the passing streetlights sending beams across the interior. "When will you decide about your employment?"

Pressure from all sides. "Why?"

"I'm curious."

Ghost panted in the front seat, watching the terrain as Moss drove. I took a cue from the dog and glanced out at the town I loved. "Mei offered an extension, so obviously they want me to stay on. That gives me leverage, especially since they know who and what I am."

"You plan to negotiate?"

"For Ghost, yes."

He fell quiet. His mind was closed off.

I squeezed his hand. "Say it."

"What?"

Corvus cleaned his feathers, making squeaking noises that grated on my nerves. "You think I should continue as a reaper."

"You *are* a reaper. You're Grim Zero."

"I'm Chloe Frost."

"You know what I mean. It's in your blood."

"Quitting would give me extra time with you."

"If we use that as our premise, then I should quit my company and relinquish my master vampire status. You should quit the veterinary clinic. If you want to do so, I am willing. We could spend the next four years, six months, and fourteen days traveling the world. Never leaving each other's side."

He was counting down the days until my soul contract was up. Didn't that say it all? "Are you picking a fight with me?"

"I'm saying your logic is flawed."

I held my response on my tongue because it wasn't very nice.

He took that as an opening to continue. "Because of our limited time, you wish to spend more of it with me, so why don't we resign from all our responsibilities and stay together until we die?"

He had me there—and I wasn't happy about it. "You'd be bored out of your mind."

"You can keep me entertained."

I leaned forward and licked his bottom lip. "I might." He caught my mouth with a fierce kiss.

When he broke it, I had to uncurl my toes. "I don't really want to see the world. I like it here in Danté's Grove, and..."

He traced a finger along my cheek. "The clinic has been your dream for a long time. You would give that up?"

Caught again. I mentally cursed. "I'd rather not."

His smile was confident. "Why do you want to quit harvesting souls? You're extremely good at it."

"It's a lot of work and it's not satisfying like helping animals."

"Death believes it's due to him."

Got me there. "Dealing with him all the time is exhausting."

"He misses you. *Her*. I believe he's truly concerned you won't renew your term."

"You two *were* talking about me."

"There has never been a time when you did not come up between us."

Good to know, but it didn't sit right with me. "Death isn't my friend and that's his fault, not mine. I wish I could say he was, but I can't."

"Are you afraid that you have feelings for him due to Grim Zero and their eternal bond?"

Reapers keepers, why was he always so spot on with his observations? "She still loves him, okay?" The words slipped out before I could catch them, and I hurried to explain. "It's not as obvious as it was initially, but I can feel it sometimes when he's around. There's this ache in my chest. She remembers things—and I, in turn, remember them, too. They had quite a romance."

He didn't like hearing it, but he'd pushed me into the admission. "Why didn't you tell me this? You didn't have to keep it a secret."

It hadn't been easy, given our connection. I could feel both his disappointment and a touch of admonishment. "Why, so you could torment yourself and pick a fight with me? What is the point of that?"

"We share everything, *that* is the point."

I could feel a matching amount of ire rising in me. "Death is my boss and *that's it*. I didn't want to upset you, and while most of the time I'm happy to share everything, there are certain things you don't need to know."

He blanched "Is that truly how you feel?"

"Do you share everything about your business or the

Undead with me? No. I don't want or need to know that stuff. I didn't tell you because I didn't want to make a big deal out of it, but now, *you* have."

His jaw firmed, causing a muscle to jump. "I want you to face what you truly are, and that is a grim reaper. You can no more deny that than I can my vampirism."

The truth of his words hit home. I bit the inside of my bottom lip, worrying it over in my mind. I wanted to tell him the truth, but I had to hold steady with my overall plan. "Did you ever wish you weren't a vampire?"

His eyes darkened. "Carrying the dragon inside me is a heavy weight. It is my destiny, however. I honor that, and those who came before me. I also respect and prize those I lead."

He loved his nest. He felt honored to be the last son in his lineage.

Grim Zero was me and I was her, just as Killion and his dragon were one and the same. There was no denying any of it. "I don't like it when we argue."

Some of the tension left his face. He sighed, then tugged me into a hug. "Nor do I. You are the sun and I am but the moon, reflecting your light."

I softened into his embrace. "You get me all annoyed at you and then you go and say something romantic like that."

He chuckled and the low sound vibrated inside my body. "I'll say nothing more about the contract or Death. Deal?"

I wrapped my arms around him as we pulled into the winding cemetery lane and Moss parked. "Deal."

When we broke apart, he pointed out the window. "How do you wish to handle this?"

It wasn't always easy for him to relinquish being leader of the pack. I appreciated his confidence in me. "I want the two of us to become invisible."

"A strategic ploy. She may still sense our presence."

"If she wants to play games, so will we. She may figure out someone is near, but perhaps she'll believe it's a ghost. The element of surprise will be our ticket to capturing her."

"You're brilliant."

I winked. "Like I said, I've been hanging around you too much."

We met Andy and Aurora at the gates. There was no storm brewing over the mostly-gone church in the distance. I was both relieved and anxious about that. I explained my plan to our counterparts.

"I like it," Aurora said. She handed each of us a small bag tied with a cord. I could feel the magic it emanated. "If you get close enough to throw this, do it. Make sure you hit her with it."

"What is it?" Andy asked.

"It will freeze her in place. Only for a few seconds, but that may be all we need." She met my gaze. "There's something else you should know. The magical grid that runs under the town has a nexus. It used to be a small area near downtown. In the past few months, it's increased in size and it's magnetic draw."

I fiddled with the spell bag. "Because of the dark artifact?"

"I think it's something else."

She looked like she might be sick. "That bad, huh? What is it?"

She swallowed hard, lifting her hood to cover her hair. "You."

"*Me?*"

"The rise in supernatural events this past year, the increase in powerful creatures finding their way here? Those aren't coincidences." Her eyes shifted to Killion, back to me. "Your ability to walk in this world and the invisible has created a portal of energy. That's why the witch is here." She fished a thick book from her bag and flipped it open to an earmarked page. Her green nail pointed to a sketch. "I read up on this type of thing. She wants to use a nexus to power up her spell. Only with that much energy will she have what she needs to trap an angel."

Killion rocked back on his heels. "So she still needs one."

"This nexus"—she gave me a disheartening look—"has the power to pull more than one entity through it. Angels, demons, ghosts, all sorts of otherworldly creatures."

"Soldiers for her war," I muttered and saw the confirmation of my guess in Aurora's gaze. "It's not only about turning shifters against vampires."

"But if the nexus is Chloe..." Andy's voice trailed off.

"Exactly." Aurora touched my arm. "Whatever you do, Chloe, do not let yourself fall into her hands."

EIGHT

ecoming invisible is always fun. The first time we'd tried it, it had unnerved me, but since then, Killion and I had used it several times to discover and follow suspects involved in our investigations.

Tonight, we had Aurora and Andy stake out the entrance and exit once more, and Killion took my hand, intertwining his fingers with mine before he used his magic to make us disappear.

There was no sigil above the gate, and I wondered if Trinity realized Aurora had dismantled the previous one and decided not to bother with another, or she hadn't noticed, and so hadn't replaced it. I asked.

"I assume the former," Aurora said, drawing her own over the gate.

That worried me. "I hope Trinity didn't grab her artifact and leave."

"We should be so lucky." Aurora saw my scowl and drew out the crystal ball. Smoke danced inside it. "She hasn't left. She needs this place to work her magic and she's consistently drawn you here for that purpose."

To my eyes, Killian and I glowed gold and silver as we moved over the rocky ground filled to the brim with dead folks.

The last ghost tour had left behind litter and I had to command Ghost to ignore a candy wrapper and cardboard box that held half eaten contents. She gave me a look that suggested I was a spoilsport.

Corvus sailed over us, flapping silently, his shadow occasionally sweeping the ground as we went. It was unusual for him to be so quiet, but he seemed to understand our mission required it. The earthbound spirits flickered in and out as we walked through the place, none paying us any mind, but none loitering either. It was almost as if they were anxious and preferred staying hidden. Perhaps because of the endless ghost tours or maybe due to Trinity.

Killion picked the center mausoleum for our lookout spot, winding an arm around me and jumping to the flat roof in an easy leap.

"You're sexy when you do that," I whispered in his ear as we settled near a crouching gargoyle that peered over the front edge to the ancient steps below. I set my sheathed weapon beside us.

The air was crisp and cool, the sky clear. A partial moon hung low, casting a bluish glow over the grounds. He chuckled and sat behind me, pulling my back against his chest. We had to remain close at all times for his magic to keep me invisible. "You're always sexy."

It was my turn to laugh. I had worn the Catwoman

suit and was glad for the warmth it generated. Ghost settled at the base of the steps leading to the crypt's double doors which were decorated with a skeleton in a topcoat for Halloween. Corvus landed on a nearby statue, becoming as unmoving as the St. Francis figure himself.

After twenty minutes, I felt antsy. Tired, too. Regardless of the suit's rubbery texture that held in my body heat, the cool air began to seep through it. I shivered against Killion.

His fingers swept my hair aside and his lips brushed my neck. Another shiver went down my spine, this one having nothing to do with the chill. "We should pay attention," I admonished.

He nibbled my earlobe, his hands trailing over my waist, my hips, down my thighs. "The psychopomp and raven will alert us."

I tilted my head to the side, allowing him greater access to my neck. He unzipped my top down to my breasts and peeled the neckline away from my skin, his fangs raking the sensitive spot on my shoulder. I pinched my thighs together where his other hand found a second sensitive spot.

Over the next few minutes, he teased me through the suit, leaving me panting and aching for more. I gripped his arm as I rubbed against his hand. He whispered taunts about what he would do to me later when we returned home.

Biting my lip, I arched against him when I tipped over into ecstasy. He slapped a hand across my mouth to smother my moan. I sank my teeth into his flesh, and he growled low and husky in my ear. The taste of his blood heightened my climax, his own pleasure teasing at me as well. That's the way it was with us. Being bonded, we experienced the sensations the other felt, causing a ricochet effect.

He didn't release his hold after the last shudder raked through me, and I licked the wound I'd left in his palm. Lifting me with ease, he turned me to face him and I saw the need in his eyes, smoldering black in the moonlight.

I want to play with your dragon, I teased.

The gold and silver sparks around us flared brighter. *He is at your command.*

Two hours later, we were mostly satiated, but I looked forward to more yet to come. What did it say about me that I was willing to make out in a cemetery surrounded by the dead?

I sighed languidly and stretched against him, thinking there was no better way to spend a boring surveillance night than like this.

A whistling, soft and breathy, brought me upright from my prone position on top of Killion. Ghost stood at attention below, facing the direction it came from. Corvus had disappeared.

Keep your magic to yourself, Killion said telepathically a heartbeat before I sent out a pulse. *This doesn't feel like our witch, but not a mundane either.*

I did as suggested, holding myself, my magic, and my breath in a vise. Ever so carefully, I adjusted my suit, but Killion stayed my hand.

The sound of muted voices, a conversation between males, floated to us. The whistling stopped and drunken laughter broke out. I spotted the teenagers from the other night, dodging headstones and tripping over gnarled, above-ground tree roots. *It's just kids. They were here last night.*

Killion didn't release my hand. *They are not mundane.*

They weren't? I'd been so focused on Trinity, I guess I hadn't noticed. *What are they?*

He sniffed the air and frowned, as if catching a whiff of something distasteful. *Ghouls.*

Me: *Like ghosts?*

Killion: *Shapeshifters who were once human and who eat the flesh of humans to stay alive. They hang out underground and around burial sites.*

Eww. *I thought they were college kids.*

Killion: *Danté's Grove is ghoul-free. Was, anyway. Can you scent them? Someone has dampened their natural odor, but it is there.*

Me: *Someone like Trinity?*

An angry nod. Drawing a deep breath, I honed in on the trio. Male sweat, liquor...

A wave of sickly sweet decaying flesh hit me and I recoiled, struggling not to gag. *That's disgusting.*

Angels, demons, now ghouls? My stomach clenched. We had seriously underestimated Trinity and her plan. *What should we do?*

Follow them.

He scooped me and the scythe up and jumped down with grace, soundless, even while carrying me. Ghost growled softly and I shushed her as he set my feet on the ground and handed me the weapon. Luckily the three were laughing and talking loud enough they didn't hear.

"Hey!" A voice came from behind me. I whirled, finding Gard standing there looking right at me. "Did you change your mind? Are you here to harvest me?"

The boys veered left, avoiding our section, picking up there gait. I put my finger to my lips to quiet him and whispered, "You can see me?"

He glanced around, noticed the males ambling off. One watched him closely and he smiled and waved. "Nothing to see here," he called to the boy. "Just talking to myself." When the ghoul glanced away, he lowered his voice and met my gaze. "Am I not supposed to?"

Killion sized him up. "Who is this?"

"Trinity's channel." Ghost sniffed at Gard's feet and he stepped back. I called her to my side. "Where is your witch?"

Gard ignored the question, his focus on Killion. "A vampire. I'm impressed."

Why, I wasn't sure, nor did I care. Neither did Killion. "How is it you can see us?" he questioned him.

"I have unique abilities." Gard gave a slight bow, his voice proud. His appearance was exactly like our previous encounter, including the garish raccoon eyes. "Not much gets past me. You've been...deliciously entertaining."

I refused to blush at the fact he was a peeping Tom and had gotten an eye-full. *It's as if he's her guard dog*, I said to Killion, *always sniffing around, marking the area.*

Yes, Killion agreed. He released his grip on me and allowed us to become visible. *His master must be close.*

I adjusted my suit, tugging the zipper higher to keep the chilly air off my chest. I wanted to demand her location, but knowing he would play games with me, I thought it smarter to interrogate him on other things first. "Tell me about the artifact."

Gard's eyes went wide. "How do you know that?"

Be careful, Killion advised. *He has no heartbeat. The ghouls did not go after him. There's something strange with this one.*

I switched gears, hoping if I kept bouncing around, I might throw him off balance and get him to divulge something errantly. "How is it she lets you wander around free?"

"You call being stuck in this place *free?*"

Was he stuck? "The sigils over the gates—are they to keep us out or you in?"

"The ones your Irish witch vaporized?" He grinned, the eyeliner cracking where crows' feet appeared. "Slick bit of magic, that was. Enraged Trinity since she's superior to all of you."

I stepped toward him and he jumped back the same amount of distance, now standing in front of the massive crypt. For someone who wanted me to harvest him, he seemed ready to run. "So they aren't to keep you imprisoned." I stuck my hand inside a pocket and touched Aurora's bespelled bag. It prickled my skin like tiny needles. Would it work on Gard if I needed to keep him here? "If she has the angel you claim you can channel, why does she need the artifact to supercharge her powers?"

He waggled a finger at me. "I'm not giving up my

secrets without your sworn promise. I'll tell you where to find her, but you have to agree to harvest me. I want it in blood, Reaper."

A blood contract? Why? What had changed? "Sounds like you don't trust me."

"I found out you have a reputation."

That was news to me. I peeked at Killion to see if he knew that to be true but he was stone-faced, giving nothing away. I confronted Gard again. "If you were to threaten me, I'm sure one of my companions would gladly kill you."

Waiting for his answer, the night fell silent, as if holding its breath. Ghost gave a low snarl. The flap of wings came from above and a shadow swept over us. Gard nervously glanced between the dog and the sky, then at Killion. I knew without looking that my partner's fangs were on display. Gard seemed to ripple in the weak moonlight, shimmering, his body becoming pixelated, then melding together once more. "She wants you, you know," he whispered under his breath. "You and the angel together could change this world and the realm of the dead."

A trickle of my magic itched to touch him, figure out what he was. I held it at bay. "She plans to use the artifact on Samhain to do just that, doesn't she?"

He tried to cover his surprise with a smile. "You *are* smart."

"Was that ever in question?" Samhain was a liminal time when the veil between worlds thinned and those with certain abilities could cross it. If Trinity combined her dark artifact, me, and the angel, I suspected she might be able to keep the veil from solidifying again, or perhaps destroy it completely.

His smile grew but he didn't answer. Pressure built behind my brows, a sickly emptiness filling my belly. Talk about end-of-the-world chaos. It was as if I could see it play out—every creature held back by the separation of worlds would be loosed on us. Ghosts, ghouls, demons...I shuddered at the thought. This wasn't simply a war between the Undead and shifters. This was a maelstrom of destruction. Apocalyptic.

I swallowed down my revulsion. The fear, however, wouldn't leave. Mentally, I ran through my options, all ranging from bad to worse. "She'll never trap Death."

Gard shifted his weight, appeared perplexed. "Sorry, you lost me."

"According to my sources, she doesn't have an angel, and I'm betting the two of you are trying to use me to get one." The idea had been circling in my brain. "The only one I know is my boss, so it stands to reason you're after him. Been there, done that. Other entities have had the same idea. It won't work."

He blinked, but offered no sign that I was on the right track. "I have no idea what you're talking about, and Trinity does, in fact, have the angel she needs."

Scary thought. "Okay, fine. I give you my word." I heard Killion in my head warn me not to make a deal. "Tell me where Trinity is and I'll send your soul on."

He brightened. "See? That wasn't so hard, was it? Where's your whatcha-ma-thingie? Your sickle. Cut your palm and then I'll do mine. We'll seal the deal."

That wasn't how it worked, but I drew the death

blade from its holder, the steel singing with its freedom. My palm heated, as did the rest of me, and I wondered if this was actually okay with the Universal order. Maybe SMG, and whoever else ran this show, realized from Gard's confession the same thing I did—if harvesting Gard stopped Trinity's plans, it was worth it.

The ground under my feet split an inch, causing a slight quake. I glanced down, back at Gard, my tattoo burning. *What's happening?*

Nothing good, came Killion's response. *Do not harvest him. This is a trick.*

Gard didn't seem to notice the mini-earthquake or the split now a foot long. "You're so close." His eyes gleamed with smug satisfaction. Trinity wasn't the only one who thought she was superior to us. "So very close."

"What are you doing?" I pointed to the jittering lawn. "Stop it."

His brows drew together and he glanced at the growing rip in the lawn between us. "I'm not doing that. I thought you were."

"Me? Why would I—" A mild shock wave hit my legs, jostling me. The ground yawned open wider. "I'm serious. Knock it off."

"I can't." His face was wary, scared. As if a sharp pain pierced his head, he grabbed it with both hands, grimacing. "It's too much."

He appeared...afflicted. There was no other term for it. Was there truly an angel and he was channeling it at that very moment? Or was Trinity doing this to him?

I couldn't stand the pain I saw in his face as he whimpered and held his head. I'd been in some dark places and knew how bad it could get, although I had no idea for sure what was happening to him.

Sometimes clarity was only a breath away, and my weapon had cut through Trinity's magic—maybe it could also cut through her hold on him, if that's what this was. "Gard," I commanded. "Look at me. I'm going to help you." Through the haze of his suffering, he peeked at me, his eyes pools of confusion and fright. "Focus on my blade."

I held it up so the steel caught moonlight. He blinked and grimaced, then zeroed in on it. One breath. Two.

By the third, the trembling stopped. The crack didn't close, but it didn't grow bigger, either. Ghost sniffed at the edge of the ragged ground.

Rivulets of sweat trickled down my back. I locked my knees, drew a relieved breath, and wiped moisture from my forehead. "You *were* doing that. How?"

"I don't...I don't know." His voice was soft, pleading. "Sometimes odd things happen when I'm stressed."

For several heartbeats, I simply stared at him as he continued to focus on the scythe. When we were all breathing easier, I decided to try again. "There's one thing I need you to clarify."

He turned wary, his gaze leaving the blade. "What?"

"If Trinity doesn't have an angel, which I know she doesn't, regardless of your claims, it means you're not a channel for any divine creature." I eyed the blade, light winking off the sharpened edge. A tumble of ideas bounced through my mind. "If there's no angel under Trinity's command, your story falls apart."

He stuttered and I braced myself for another earthquake. "I told you, she does. I'm the channel for him."

I stepped closer. "What's his name? This angel?"

He once again backed away, keeping out of reach. "It's...uh...Drathvad...iel. Drathvadiel. That's right."

"You're making that up," Killion said.

"No." He waved his hands. While the ground didn't tremble, the split inched silently toward him. "I'm not. That's what she calls him. I swear it."

I pointed the tip of the blade at his chest, considering and discarding the idea he simply wanted the weapon and its power. He wouldn't be the first to try and steal the scythe, but why did he keep backing away? I had half a mind to swipe him with it and see if he was actually here in flesh and blood. "Tell us the truth."

The crack widened. "I *am*." He looked pained as he brought his hands together in a prayer gesture at his chest. His voice turned whiney. "You have to believe me."

Be careful, Killion warned.

I held my ground. "It's not an angel, is it?" This whole time, we'd been focused on the wrong type of power and now I was sure of this small distinction. "She's snagged a demon. How powerful is he?"

His hands fell to his side. His beseeching expression disappeared, one of annoyance taking his place. "You don't want to know."

"Must not be very, if she managed to trap him in that artifact and still needs me to complete her plans."

Indignant, he huffed. "Don't be stupid. This demon is clever and a dynamic force. One to be reckoned with."

And if I had to guess, I was staring right at him. "How did she bind him to the artifact?"

Another huff. "She's skilled in dark magic."

"And you're not?"

"What?" More indignation. "I only want to leave this world, to not be a part of her twisted plans. It's all gone so...wrong."

A chill swept over my skin. In the shadows, I sensed Katarina and Harlow joining the party. Killion eased next to me, his shoulder brushing mine. "Because you had your own plans, didn't you?" he asked quietly.

The being in front of us continued to play dumb. "I just want to go home."

Sure he did. "Where is she?" If I killed him, I wouldn't get answers. If I didn't... "Give her up."

"I can't." He shook his head. "All I can do is get you where you need to be."

The words didn't make sense but then Corvus swooped down, blaring a screeching croak as his war cry. At the same moment, the ground convulsed, the soil roiling under my feet. Killion jerked me out of the way of the fissure, grass and clay tumbling into it. From the yawning maw came a stench that reminded me of chemistry class. Rotten eggs.

Sulfur.

Ghost morphed into her psychopomp. Corvus aimed his claws at Gard—and went right through him.

Gard's image wavered and blinked out as Ghost lunged.

I stumbled as the quake intensified, only Killion keeping me on my feet. The base of the gargoyle cracked and the statue listed to one side, then to the other as the entire patch of burial ground pitched under our feet.

"Ghost!" I screamed. "Look out!"

Corvus lit into the air again, Katarina and Harlow came running, covering the expanse so fast they were a blur. Harlow snatched at the dog and leaped, but not before the gargoyle fell and knocked both of them to the ground.

The shaking stopped. The statue landed on the stone steps in front of the mausoleum door. It cracked with a sharp blast and a shard sliced across my cheek. I gasped at the sight of the wound on my dog's side.

The stinging pain caused my eyes to tear. Rage at Gard's tricks roared through me. "Ghost!"

She whined and rolled an eye toward me as I ran and dropped to my knees next to her. I skimmed gentle fingers over the blood-soaked fur and she flinched when I touched a tender rib. Her flesh had been flayed open by one of the statue's wings and bone peeked through. Instantly, I went into vet mode. "You're going to be okay," I assured her. Killion shed his coat and stripped off his shirt, handing it to me. I gently but firmly pressed it into her side to stem the blood. Harlow took the jacket and laid it over her lower half for warmth. "I'm going to get you fixed up."

Harlow buried her fingers in the dog's thick neck hair, stroking her. "I will help."

She'd filled in for me once at the clinic. Gratitude at her offer swamped me. I couldn't exactly call one of my doctors or Nita to assist.

"Can you morph?" Killion asked the psychopomp.

"No." I shook my head. "If she does, her broken rib could pierce her heart. We have to fix her this way."

Killion slit his wrist with a fang and I moved the compress so he could drip blood into the wound. It would help, but she still needed stitches. He, Katarina, and Harlow carried her to the limo and gently finagled her inside.

Aurora and Andy joined us. Aurora placed a hand on my shoulder. "What happened? Will she be okay?"

I filled her in through gritted teeth. Tears threatened to spill down my cheeks and I blinked them away. "I will kill them both," I snarled, Ghost's whimpers echoing in my ears. Moss assisted to make sure she was as comfortable as possible. "Gard is a demon and they're working together. I'm sure of it."

Aurora's clasp on me tightened. "A demon? Well, that changes everything."

"If it's the last thing I do," I swore. "I will make them wish they'd never met me."

NINE

An hour later, Ghost's broken rib was on the mend, and her side had been cleaned and stitched. I commanded her not to shift until I was sure it would do no damage.

Harlow sent me to the office where Killion, Katarina, Aurora, and Andy waited, saying she would keep an eye on Ghost and clean up. I gave Ghost's head a kiss before I slipped out, knowing she was in good hands. She closed her eyes and was instantly asleep, her customary snores granting a moment of relief.

I stalked into the room that had once belonged to my parents. Never in all their days could they have imagined the group gathered there. "I want their heads," I said with calm detachment. "Trinity, her coven, Gard or whatever his name is."

"I've alerted SMG that we are dealing with a demon." Killion took my hand and drew me to him. "You figured it out."

"Makes more sense," Aurora said. "Trinity doesn't

seem the type to mess with higher order beings, only lower ones."

I plunked on the edge of what had been my dad's desk and was now Dr. O'Leary's. "Yeah, on the scale of good and evil, Darth Vader is on the evil side."

"Darth Vader?" Andy asked.

"Gard was making up a name for the supposed angel and it sounded like a terrible configuration of Darth Vader."

"Ah, a Star Wars fan." He nodded as if this was a virtue. "You can't miss going with The Chosen One."

"Harry Potter is The Chosen One," I argued.

He gave a nonchalant shrug. "In your world of witches and wizards, I guess."

"It's a classic story trope," Katarina growled. "Can we get back to the matter at hand?"

"Sorry." I rubbed my eyes, feeling much older than my twenty-five years. "We need a new plan."

The enforcer gave a nod. "The witch can't be that hard to sniff out. Why can't the shifter track her?"

The shifter in question scoffed. "She's avoided capture for hundreds of years. Why do you think that is, bloodsucker?"

Annnd...this was why bringing the Undead and shifters together seemed easier on paper than it was in real life.

Aurora's hackles were up and when Katarina snarled at Andy, she raised her fingers, a spell crackling on the ends of them. "Try it."

"Enough." Killion's command was quiet yet dangerous. Neither the witch, nor the vampire, appreciated it, but both backed down.

Andy grinned. "Fighting my battles for me?" he teased Aurora. She flicked her magic at him and he winced. "Ow, that hurt."

"Trinity possesses rare and highly refined power," Killion stated, ignoring them. "She's getting stronger by the day. She has a demon, and possibly ghouls and ghosts at her disposal. As Chloe said, we need a new plan. There will be no sneaking up on her or Gard." He was motionless, though vibrating with unspent anger. "I suspect he is actually a hybrid of some type. He was trying to bind Chloe to him by blood this time."

I grumbled curses under my breath. "Sneaky little jerk."

"A hybrid like a Nephilim?" Andy visibly shuddered. "I thought those were myths."

"Nephilim are halflings. Human-angel or human-demon combinations," Killion told him. "Rare, but not as rare as this entity. From the feel of his magic, I suspect he's both. I couldn't put my finger on it immediately, but after seeing what he can do, I'm sure of it. You can imagine the clash of good and evil inside such a being."

"There's a legend about one," Aurora spoke up, scrolling through something on her phone. "I was scanning more of my older texts, searching for more info about the *Key of Holumdra*." She stopped and nodded. "There. That's it. Ragriel, an angel-demon mix, considered by most to be a myth, but one of the original keepers of the text, along with that coven, is claimed to have captured him.

They wanted to control the living and the dead, and stalked cemeteries, using him to raise bodies." She glanced up. "It apparently didn't go well for them. It's said he became like smoke and struck each and every member down."

A light went on in Killion's eyes. "When I was young, my father spoke of the *terror of the night*—a genderless shapeshifting entity who moved like smoke and fog and could kill and raise the dead for his own purposes. Could that be the same creature?"

"A necromancer?" I asked.

"Not in the traditional sense." He crossed his arms and frowned. "Both the living and the dead were tools for him to enter the Otherworld realms. He roamed all of them according to the stories, seeking a home but never finding it. Nobody would accept him as one of theirs."

I snapped my fingers. "He wants to go home. That's what Gard keeps saying."

"Ragriel is here?" Aurora's voice was a screech. "In Danté's Grove?"

"Along with ghouls." Killion nodded. "There were three at the cemetery tonight."

"Trinity has drawn them here?" She clicked her tongue at his second nod. "My citywide security meter has not alerted me to them, but then, I never expected any to show up." She had placed a spell over the entire area to inform her of what was going on magically. Newcomers, those leaving, and any disturbances that signified problems, which was why she'd felt my magic during my astral travel adventure. She was better than any of the neighborhood apps out there. "The flesh of those they eat gives ghouls information. If she's their master, then she gains that knowledge."

"They are controlled only by their queen, but the two could be in league together."

Aurora paled. "Do you know who they've been snacking on? I've seen no disturbances in Shepherd's Rest, have you?"

"That graveyard holds importance to her." He stared at the top of one of the desks, not seeing it. "But she doesn't want to call mundane attention to it. If they disturbed graves and law enforcement was called in, it could set back her plans. They must be eating elsewhere."

"I'll check into it," Katarina volunteered. "Chloe can question the local ghosts. Maybe between the two of us, we can get a handle on where she's hiding. They may be less loyal than this hybrid demon who believes he's The Chosen One."

"That's a good idea," I said, dropping into my dad's old chair. Just sitting in it comforted me. "*If* I can get any of the earthbound spirits to talk to me." Most tended to run when they saw me coming because they didn't want to move on. Their reasons for staying varied from being bent on revenge, believing their relatives needed them, or even because they were scared about where they'd spend their afterlife.

"Maybe we should call off the Halloween party," Andy suggested.

Aurora moved closer, resting a ringed hand on his arm as she nodded. "Agreed. The potential for a feud is high and would distract from the real evil going down."

Everyone glanced at Killion. A muscle in his jaw jumped. "There will always be someone trying to stop a union between us," he said. "I will not give this witch"—he spit the word and Aurora tensed—"the satisfaction of succeeding. The party will be held; we will prevent Trinity from harming anyone. I give you all my word."

While he kept his emotions under a tight lock and key, I felt them beneath his shield. Felt his dragon raging at what had happened and the trouble Trinity might yet cause.

Harlow peeked in. "The psychopomp is sleeping deeply and healing quickly. Is there anything else I can do?"

I rubbed my eyes and pasted on what I hoped passed for a genuine smile. "No, thank you. She should be back to her normal self by morning."

"I overheard what you said," she addressed Killion, filling out the doorway. "I assigned three of our best trackers on the hybrid's trail. It appears he has disappeared, and they have found nothing but an odd, hazy magic in the cemetery. Should they expand their search area?"

Killion paused, as if considering it, then shook his head. "Not until I know more."

She bobbed her head once and disappeared into the back again.

"By the way," Aurora said, "while you were working on Ghost, I uncovered an entry in an older spellcaster almanac that references what I believe coincided with Trinity's birth. The details are scant, and it was centuries ago, but I'm pretty sure she was born under a blood moon, fulfilling a prophecy that was notated in it."

"Of course she was." I leaned back in the chair. "And?"

"Trinity's mother, father, and twin brother died in a fire when she was a few days old. She was found outside in the yard unharmed. No one ever figured out how she escaped, but she bore a mark on her neck—some claimed it was a demon who saved her and the mark was his."

I sat forward. "Is it Gard—this Ragriel? Did he save her?"

"I can't be sure, but that would make him *her* master. Not the other way around."

"She said something that first night about it." I recalled her words and realized they made sense now. "'*My master will protect me from your blade, no matter what. He sent me here. To find you. To test you. To start a war that even you can't stop.*' She didn't answer me about who he was, though."

Aurora brought up a photo on her phone and handed the device to me. "See the death date listed on these markers?"

I zoomed in. "What about it?"

"It's the same as those listed on the ones in Shepherd's Rest."

I glanced up. "Tilly and what's-his-name?"

"There are three—a mother, father, and unnamed son."

"But Trinity was born in Europe, wasn't she? Not here."

"A small village in what was at that time part of the

Russian Empire." Aurora reached for the cell. "A coincidence?"

Killion shook his head. "There must be a connection, a reason. Continue to look into it."

"How can Gard be both angel and demon?" I couldn't wrap my mind around it. "I'd hate to be inside his head."

Andy chuckled. "Like the proverbial angel on one shoulder and devil on the other, except his is literal. That would suck."

"We all wrestle with our inner beasts." Killian's tone offered no pity. "It merely makes him an unstable enemy with unknown depths to his power. We must tread carefully."

Aurora looked as if a lightbulb had gone off above her head. She hitched a hip on the corner of my mom's old desk and snapped her fingers. "Maybe that's why he needed Trinity. Because of her power and mastery, she helps him control his."

Killion considered it. "Could that be why he saved her from the fire? Did he realize, even then, that she possessed the right kind to help him with his?"

"He probably started the fire," Aurora said. "To make her indebted to him. It's a symbiotic relationship, neither of them holding the upper hand."

"Do you think my assumption is correct?" I asked. "That they plan to tear down the wall between the visible and invisible worlds on Halloween?"

"It's a good theory." She paled more. "They could unleash all manner of evil entities into this world. None of us will survive, even with our magics."

We fell silent and Killion's protectiveness plowed into me like a linebacker. It was nearly suffocating, but I endured it because I understood how he felt. My magic was probably doing the same to him, trying to protect him from the potential threat.

Andy stiffened right before I heard a knock at the back door. All of us went on alert, and then Harlow's voice filtered through. The second voice was also one I recognized—Pepper, the coyote shifter who was in my frenemy category.

Exhausted, I reluctantly hauled myself to my feet, the rest of the group trailing after me as I exited the office to follow the voices.

"Sorry, Master," Harlow said to Killion as we came upon them. "The shifter and her sister are requesting to speak to you and the grim. I told her now was not a good time."

He faced the coyote female, another coming up behind her slowly. They were both short and lean, Pepper dark haired while her sister's was copper colored. They wore matching necklaces. "What is it you want?"

Pepper's nervous gaze bounced between him and Andy, then landed on me. "My grandmother was an elder in our clan for fifty years. She died last week and we buried her on our private property. Her grave has been disturbed; her body was..." She hiccupped, lips pressing into a hard line before she took a breath and continued. "Desecrated. Her spirit bag is missing. If she doesn't have that..." Her voice trailed off again. Tears shone in her eyes. "We request your services. Can you help us?"

I hesitated, unsure what I could do.

Her sister's expression was set in cold rage. "She was revered and loved! Who would do this? It is sacred land." She shook with emotion. "She cannot cross to the afterlife without her spirit bag."

Pepper's next words caught on a sob and she tried to suppress it. Coarse gray and black fur sprouted on the side of her neck, and I instinctively tensed. "She'll walk among the ghosts, never finding peace."

My thoughts spun as everyone glanced my way. I didn't have time, nor the energy for this, but Pepper's distress had me moving forward to take her hand. "Do you have any ideas who might have done it?"

She shook her head, tears slipping down her cheeks. "Chloe, they *ate* pieces of her!" Her free hand went to her mouth to hold back another sob. "I saw teeth marks."

"The ghouls," I muttered.

She drew back with a look of horror. "Ghouls?"

"Your grandmother wasn't embalmed, was she?"

She shook her head, seeming more confused. "It's against our beliefs." Her attention speared Killion. "Is the ghoul queen here as well?"

His brows lifted. "What do you know of her?"

"Only that she is reticent to become involved with your kind."

Smart.

His words were clipped. "She stays south, avoids my territory, as per our agreement."

This sounded like a story I needed to hear, but not now. "Why?"

"The Undead have no use for those who feast on the flesh of humans."

"You drink their blood," Andy said. "Not all that different."

Killion's upper lip twitched and his fangs flashed. "We are nothing alike."

Moving surreptitiously, I touched his shoulder. "Could that be the war she meant? Not what Gard, er, Ragriel, told me about you and the shifters?"

"Between the Undead and the ghouls?" Katarina snorted. "No contest there."

"Unless the hybrid is fueling them," Killion countered. "We need more information. I will contact Death."

"In the meantime," I told Pepper, "go home and honor your grandmother. I'll come by tomorrow and see if I can speak to her ghost, if she *is* hanging around." She might be able to tell us more. "I know where to find the probable suspects and we'll handle it, okay?"

Pepper's sister widened her stance, glaring at me. "*We* will handle them. Tell us where to find them."

Anger and determination rolled off her in equal waves. I admired her spunk and understood how devastating this had to be for them, but I couldn't risk them rushing in to confront those in Shepherd's Rest without evidence they were our culprits.

Plus, if the ghouls were tied to Trinity, I needed to know what their part was in her plan.

"Please." I squeezed Pepper's hand and looked deeply into her eyes. She'd been under my control once and I noted her flinch, fearing I was about to use compulsion on her. I was so tired even my eyeballs ached, and I certainly didn't have the energy, even if I'd wanted to.

"Give me until tomorrow night. I will get you the answers you need."

Although the words felt hollow on my tongue—I'd been making a lot of promises lately that I hadn't followed through on—she nodded. "Thank you."

"Andy will go with you and help you set up surveillance at your burial grounds to make sure they don't return and disturb anyone else, okay?"

She threw her arms around my neck. "I knew you would help us." Her sister protested, but between Pepper and Andy, they managed to get her to leave with them.

I slumped into a plastic chair in the break room. I'd had four hours of sleep in the past day and my vision was starting to blur. "Katarina, you're on ghoul duty. Aurora, you stay on Trinity, see if you can find more about her and Ragriel. Killion and I will speak to SMG and Death and see what we can learn from them regarding his powers. We'll reconvene tomorrow."

"And me?" Harlow asked.

Killion pointed at the connecting area where the kennels were. "Assist Moss to get the dog in the car. Then put out the word to everyone in our nest—find the witch, but do not touch her."

She dipped her head. "Yes, Master."

Once Ghost was snoring on the seat across from us in the limo, we drove home, the sky pink with the rising sun.

My hair still smelled of sulfur.

TEN

I slept ten hours. When I woke, I scarfed down three boiled eggs and four waffles, while chastising Killion in between bites for allowing me to sleep so long.

"You needed it," was his response.

He was right, of course, but I still felt like I had let everyone down by giving into my exhaustion. "Pepper is expecting me to get to the bottom of her issue."

"Andy has explained our situation and reassured her we are looking into it. She and her sister will meet us at the private cemetery when we're ready."

Ghost was up and running around in her normal size. She bit into Killion's pant leg and tugged, trying to get him to play with her. His landline in the living room rang and Pennyworth popped out from the kitchen to answer it.

Killion removed Ghost's teeth from his designer slacks and retrieved one of her balls from a basket of toys. He tossed it down the hall to the bedroom and she scrambled for it. Pennyworth handed him the phone, announcing Harlow wished to speak to him. "She tried your cell, but said she got your voicemail."

As Killion took her call, the butler returned to the dining room, pointing at my cup. "Refill?"

"Yes, please."

While he topped me off, I peeked to make sure Killion was out of earshot. "May I ask a favor?"

"Of course. A special request for your next meal?"

"No, something else. The seamstress who made the dresses for me that Killion favors—would she have time or an interest in talking to me about a wedding gown?"

Pennyworth nearly dropped the carafe. "I'm sure she would be honored."

"Can you give me her number or set up an appointment so I can talk to her? I have some ideas. This has to stay a secret, okay? No one but you and I can know."

He brightened, shooting a glance toward his master pacing in the living room. "Absolutely. She doesn't use modern technology for communication. I'll visit her tonight while the two of you are gone."

The sassy Papillon-mix hopped into my lap and demanded a slice of veggie bacon. Being the sucker I am, and so relieved to see her healed, I gave it all to her. "Thank you."

He bowed and zipped his lips with his fingers as Killion returned. "I'm pleased to be of service."

He disappeared into the kitchen and Killion sunk into his chair.

I sipped the fresh coffee. "Bring me up to speed."

He looked tired, and I wondered if he needed blood.

"SMG and Death have information on our hybrid." He slid a blue folder across the table to me. "As suspected, he's known as Ragriel. His heritage is unknown. SMG has been trying to catch him for some time. Once, a long time ago, they managed to do it, until an unidentified entity freed him. Our theory about him saving Trinity in order to use her powers to control his appears probable."

I scanned through the facts while I petted Ghost. "Are they going to help us eliminate him?"

"He cannot be eliminated per se, only imprisoned."

"All his talk about wanting to go home—what a joke."

Killion swirled the liquid in his glass. "He may actually consider the underworld to be his home."

"The underworld, as in hell?"

A shrug. "Different cultures have varying names for it. His previous imprisonment was in a more, how should I say it, *divine* place. I imagine for a half-demon, that could be his version of hell."

"Soul Management Group has prisons?"

"The details have never been shared with me, but I imagine even Eden had its drawbacks."

"Yeah, like snakes." I flipped over the top page and scanned the next, listing dozens of crimes against humans as well as supernaturals they suspected him of. "He has quite a rap sheet. Plenty of fire and brimstone, genocide, famine... He sounds like the famed Four Horsemen all wrapped up in one. Why doesn't his angelic side ever kick in?"

"Unknown. This is why we must be extremely careful."

"Trinity is keeping him in line and he can't be killed.

If I take her out"—my stomach clenched—"there will be nobody to keep him from wreaking havoc."

"There is one option."

"Does Mei have a plan?"

"Read the summary on the final page."

I munched on a slice of apple, flipping to the last sheet of paper. It read like a law school summary, dry and full of technical terms. My gaze caught on a sentence and I glanced up. "No."

Killion's face was as dark as a thunderstorm about to unleash itself. "I'm afraid so. Grim Zero has been the only entity to capture him. That must be done before you harvest Trinity in order to keep the natural balance in order."

My stomach clenched harder. I set Ghost on the rug and she ran off to grab a squeaky toy. "And how exactly am I supposed to do that?"

"By trusting me. I have a ploy."

Of course he did. My stomach relaxed a bit. "Care to fill me in?"

"I've been over every possible scenario." He still looked like he wanted to destroy something. Or someone. "My plan is the only way."

My smile fell. "I'm not going to like it, am I?"

"It will require you to stand down."

"*What?* It says right here that I'm the only one who can capture him."

"Correction." He held up a finger. "You're the only entity they've ever sent after him. There's a difference, and I believe with the combined forces of the supernaturals I'm gathering, we'll be able to do it for you."

"You think I'm going to let you handle this alone?" My magic rose with my anxiety, tingling my skin. "We're partners, remember?"

"Death and I have discussed it—we cannot risk you becoming his pawn in this game. Aurora agrees. You're a nexus for power, and in your past incarnation, you didn't face him and Trinity *together*."

"They've never faced *us* together."

He reached for my hand but I drew away, frightened at the idea of him taking on a demon hybrid and this witch.

His thundercloud expression turned annoyed. "I know this goes against your wishes, but if they were to collect you and your blood with its tremendous power, they could destroy this world."

"I won't let them." My food turned sour in my belly, even as I said the words. The images of Armageddon filled my brain once more. "But there's something you should know."

"What?"

"When she dragged me to Shepherd's Rest with bilocation, somehow, her magic managed to scratch me."

He frowned. "You weren't physically there. How could she?"

"I don't know. She never touched me. It felt like her magic was raking me, though, and I ended up with visible scratches while my physical body was still safe at the clinic."

"Did you bleed?"

I shook my head. "They were fine, white lines.

Similar to when Ghost's nails are too long and she leaves a mark on my skin."

A measure of relief crossed his face. "Chloe, it's too risky for you to go near her."

"What am I supposed to do, sit here and drink wine? Read a book?" The dog raced over and launched herself into my lap once more, her stuffed penguin losing filling from both ends. "I'm supposed to play with Ghost while you and the others are out there risking your lives?"

"Ghost is a part of my plan."

I threw up my hands. "No. That's not happening. We're a team, you and I. If you go, I go."

He studied the family ring on his finger rather than meeting my eyes. "We *are* a team, but sometimes it is in the best interest of all involved if only one of us takes the lead."

"And that's you?"

"Yes." His hard gaze met mine and in it I saw his utter remorse at pulling the boss card with me. I also saw his resolution. "This isn't the time to be headstrong about your role. The odds are stacked against us because of who you are. You must understand that."

My uniqueness was legendary. I was *the* grim; that alone made me unequaled in the supernatural department. I could take souls and my necromancy allowed me to resurrect them as well. My blood made me the most rare and exclusive supernatural the world had ever seen. Which was why I needed to be part of this. "I'm the only one who has the level of power to match Trinity and her hybrid. You know that."

"I do, but if they were to get hold of you, no force in

this world or beyond will be able to stop them. Not even Death. I could lose you forever to the dark side."

"I hear they have cookies."

He didn't smile.

Leverage. He used it all the time in his daily Undead life with his vampires and clients. Now he was using it with me. "We are *incatusa sufletum*." I swallowed the pit in my throat. "No one can split us apart."

"I believed that to be true, but Death claims that Ragriel could break our bond. Could break *you*. It nearly happened before when he didn't have Trinity's power boosting his."

His words sank in and I felt my meal threaten to come back up. "With Death and Grim Zero?"

His nod was stiff.

Those two had been the original *incatusa sufletum*. They'd believed nothing and no one could sever their soul bond. If Ragriel had nearly done that...

I jammed my fork into the top of the table. "Nothing can break our bond."

"He and Trinity could damage your soul to such an extreme you would never recover. You would, in essence, be lost to all of us and bound to them instead. *Forever*," he added with emphasis.

That gave me pause. "There has to be something I can do. You're not equipped to face them without me, even if you call on every supernatural in the world."

Faster than I could blink, he gripped my hand, bringing it to his lips. "Trust me."

The message behind those words vibrated inside my bones. My blood hummed with his plea. Something was going on that I couldn't put my finger on. Not only his protectiveness and damnable logic, something more. "I always do."

"You rang?" Death popped into the room and leaned his huge frame on the back of a dining chair. The wood groaned. His hair was loose and a shimmering gold tonight, and he wore black from head to toe. "What did I miss?"

Grim Zero stirred and I shut her down. "I have to be in on the fight with Trinity and Rag."

He threw his head back and his laugh rang too loud in my ears. It ceased just as quickly. "No."

I waited for him to argue more, but he simply looked at me, expressionless.

"I don't accept that."

"I don't care." He dragged out the chair and collapsed into it with a huff. "What's your strategy for tonight?" he asked Killion.

That he would defer to the master vampire surprised me, but between all of us, Killion *was* the most calculating and clever.

I wasn't about to let him off the hook, however. Releasing Killion's hand, I grabbed two slices of toast, cut in perfect triangles. I'd need my strength for whatever came next and my determination to keep everyone safe overcame my queasiness. "First, tell me about this angel-demon hybrid."

ELEVEN

"You know what I know." Death eyed the remnants of my meal. He swiped a triangle of buttered toast from the corner of my plate. "He causes mayhem whenever he's loose, but this round, he's been underground so long, SMG sort of wrote him off. You and I have a particular history with him."

"You and I worked together to trap him. We can do it again. He has weaknesses." I thought about the afflicted way he'd acted the night before. "I need to know what those are and how to capitalize on them."

Death munched on the toast. "Since we did that previously in order to lock him up, he'll be prepared. We have to come at this with fresh ideas, not try to repeat what you and I did before. He's too smart for that."

"But he's part angel and you—" He hated it when I called him on his wings. "You should have insight into his mind."

"He's *not* like me." Death was quicker this time, nabbing the remaining toast. He chewed triumphantly.

"Crossbreeds are not divine beings. They're as rare as they come, but they are abominations. Supernatural mongrels who have no place in this world. He and I have as much in common as you and a slug."

Crossbreed? Mongrel? "He's not an animal, and even if he were, you're being offensive."

"Get over it," he growled.

"My strategy of combining the skills of the Undead with those of the other supernaturals in this area will work," Killion interceded, ignoring the way Death and I glared at each other.

There was no track record to prove it, though. I finished my food and wiped off my sticky fingers. "Rag and Trinity have tricks, but I don't know how smart they are. We destroy the artifact and that alone will weaken her, which in turn will weaken them both, right?"

The corner of Killion's mouth twitched, and I could see him suppressing a smile. I was his student, as much as Death's employee. "That was my first thought, as well. We need to determine what the artifact is and where she's hiding it. I've called for a meeting between the Undead and shifter hierarchy. We need a party to search for this object."

"It's not at the church, right?"

He shook his head. "Katarina has confirmed it."

The clouds and lightning were another show. "She'll have it close so she can protect it." I smacked Death's hand when he reached for another triangle. Pennyworth had placed three types of jam on the table, and I smothered mine with strawberry. "Which leads us back to the fact *I* need to find her. The ghosts can help. No one can hide from them. No matter how stealthy the other trackers are, she might sense them and realize what they're after."

Killion surprised me by agreeing. "The ghosts would be more efficient and less noticeable, since she seems to have stationed her headquarters in the cemetery."

"I'll do it," Death said.

While ghosts often ran from me, there were always those who wanted to chat. Not one would stick around if they saw him coming, however. "Don't be ridiculous."

"You really think they'll talk to you?" he scoffed.

"If I make them an offer they can't refuse, they'll help," I insisted.

Death fingered a knife, turning it over and over. "I can't allow it. We'll use the other necromancer, the witch."

I cursed under my breath. He had me there. Aurora was able to talk to the dead as well. "Trinity and Rag pose no threat to me if all I'm doing is recruiting a couple ghosts."

He shook his head. "Too dangerous. They could show up."

I mimicked his head shake and tapped the table. "But now we know who Ragriel is and what they're up to. Their tricks have failed so far, and they've showed their hand. We know the players involved and their master strategy. I'll bet my leather boots Trinity is worried. Think about it—she has one chance to make her plan work, and it has to be done at midnight when the veil is thinnest, otherwise, she'll have to wait another year. In that amount of time, the odds are I will track her down and harvest her. Rag has already failed to capture me once. She won't risk letting him try again. All she's been doing is testing me, testing us. To find our strengths and weaknesses so she doesn't blow her big chance. She knows if any of this goes sideways, she'll lose the respect and loyalty of her coven, and she needs them. Regardless, she can't trap me now because I know what she's trying to do."

Killion's lips quirked again, and he hid his smile behind a sip of wine. Death stared at me, trying to sort through everything I'd said. He threw out an argument anyway—I expected nothing less. "Aurora can talk to the ghosts. You don't need to be there."

"She can't make the deal with them that I can."

He gave me a smug look. "And what is that?"

"That I won't send them to the afterlife."

He snorted. "That's part of your job."

"Not for long, unless you cooperate with me on this." I pushed back my plate and held his disgruntled gaze. "I'll quit right now if you don't concede."

"You can't. Your agreement—"

"Wanna try me?" I tapped the side of my head. "Grim Zero lives up here, or have you forgotten? She was created for this job, but I wasn't. Neither you, nor Mei, want Chloe Frost to continue as a reaper—you want *her*. Thing is, Grim Zero wants me to sign on for another year. It's what she lives for—seeing you, harvesting souls, speaking to the dead. Unfortunately for you, it's a package deal and I hold the cards."

His glare held predatory intent. "You are such a pain in my—"

"She's absolutely correct," Killion said, his smile breaking free and making me feel like a prized student, even as his protectiveness made him yearn to loose his dragon on my boss. "Grim Zero can advise us, even if we have to keep Chloe safe."

Death bristled and stewed, continuing to throw out arguments, but finally gave a gruff nod when none of them held water.

Killion cleared his throat with a growl. "Just to clarify, not *you*, not *SMG*. Grim Zero trapped Ragriel previously."

"And it cost her," he growled. "Us."

"I understand that, but she's not lost to you," I argued. "Others have weakened your bond, but it's still there. I can feel it."

His gaze dropped, then rose, full of sadness. "That doesn't mean you can handle him."

"Actually, it does." I used my foot to touch Killion's leg under the table. I refused to break eye contact with Death, but I wanted my partner to know I had this under control. That he had taught me well when it came to negotiating. That I was still his, not Death's, even if Grim Zero loved the angel. "I'm not only your best bet, I'm your only sure one."

His tone mocked me, yet I caught a hint of challenge. "Is that so?"

You bet your robes it is. "I'm good at this job because of who I am, so let me do it."

Fiery daggers from Death. I held his gaze, my skin pebbling with his magic blasting me. Even Killion's protection wasn't enough to completely keep him at bay.

When he saw I wouldn't back down, he rested his elbows on the wood, resigned. A sight I rarely saw. "You *are* good at this. SMG wants you to keep reaping because of that very reason."

"Then it's settled." Killion started to rise. "We'll head to Shepherd's Rest—"

"Not so fast, fang boy." Death held up a hand, ignoring Killion's snarl at the nickname. So much for their newfound friendship. "Chloe has something else to say, don't you?"

I sucked in a breath. *Busted.*

I had kept my true desires hidden, in case he'd been messing around in my head. I wasn't the only one who understood leverage when it came to him and SMG.

Everything hinged on what happened next and I played dumb, praying this would work. "Nope. I'm ready to go."

I bolted out of the chair and he pointed, his power over me freezing me in my tracks. "Sit."

Killion tensed, ready to intervene. Fighting Death's magic, I gritted my teeth, but did as directed, letting Killion know with a flick of my eyes that I was okay. So far, so good. I couldn't make this look easy or as if I'd been planning this since I'd found out about my shortened life expectancy. "I don't know what you're talking about."

"Don't you?" Death's smile was lazy, confident, yet still held that predatory gleam. "Wasn't there another negotiation floating around in that crazy brain of yours?"

He *had* been reading my mind. Hopefully, all my arguments and justifications for not re-signing with SMG had done the trick.

Steady, my grim counterpart warned. *Don't rush or he'll know what you're up to.*

Although I'd absorbed as much of Grim Zero as I could—including her overwhelming emotions and intense personality—there were times she continued to feel like a separate entity. One thing I knew for sure, she would *never* quit this job. She'd been created for the very purpose of harvesting souls and protecting Death. He needed her. Needed *me*.

Death's magic tickled my throat. My jaw clenched, trying to hold back the words he wanted me to spill. I pinched my lips, gripping the edge of the table.

"Stop it," Killion bared his teeth. "She is not your toy."

Death paid no attention to him. "Say it."

I swallowed hard. "Why? So you can gloat?"

"I gave you the opportunity to discuss this with me like a mature, responsible adult. To trust me enough that I would hear you out, and quite possibly assist you with your negotiations with Mei. As per normal, you assumed the worst. Didn't talk to me about your concerns."

"Because I knew you'd say no."

He feigned hurt. "I thought we were friends."

"Your definition of friendship and mine are very different."

He grimaced, then ran a hand over his face. He kicked back from the table and studied the chandelier. Finally, a tortured sigh whooshed out of him. "Fine. I can do better."

My heart pinched at the sudden and unexpected gentleness in his words and the raw expression on his face. There had always been these two sides of him—the boss and the broken angel who missed his partner and yearned for her acceptance and camaraderie with such longing it stole my breath.

All of it made sense. He'd lowered himself to befriend Killion so he could be close to me—*her.*

"I can, too," I admitted, although I wasn't sure how. As soon as I said it the vise around my throat and jaw released. This was my opening, but I couldn't act eager. I closed my eyes for dramatic effect and clenched my hands into fists. I let silence hang between us as if it took every ounce of my being to say the next words. "If you let me take down Trinity and Ragriel,"—I swallowed and stared at him—"I'll sign on for another year."

The smugness increased tenfold, but the genuine happiness in his eyes made him look like I'd given him the best gift in the world. "That wasn't so hard, was it? Where's your phone? Let's get that extension to your employment agreement signed."

I held up a finger. "I have a condition."

His nostrils flared, wariness creeping back in. "Of course you do, but you're not in the driver's seat on this one."

But I was. "I want five extra years on my soul contract."

"Only five?" Death winked at Killion, acting buddy-buddy again. "She's learned a lot from you, bloodsucker, but she still lacks your ability to milk a situation for maximum benefit."

I felt Killion pushing against my mind, willing me to open the channel between us. I couldn't—Death might eavesdrop. I leaned forward ever so slightly. "The number just went up to ten."

A chuckle. "That's more like it." No one reveled in a challenge more than he did. This was sport for him. He grinned, his Aussie accent thickening. "Seven, and you'll train two new grims to help with your expanded area and fill in while you're off to Romania."

Train rookies? Expanded area? I bit my bottom lip to keep from calling him a name. Had he expected this and created a counteroffer ready to go? "Ten or nothing, and my death will not trigger Killion's."

The master vampire came out of his seat. "Chloe!"

Death chuckled. "He'll off himself if you die, so it's a moot point."

Not if I could convince him otherwise. "I want it in writing."

"Do not do this," Killion urged. "He's correct—I will not walk this earth without you by my side."

It killed me, but I had to ignore him. I desperately wanted to tell him to trust me, but I knew that would tip my hand. "You're all I care about. Please, let me do this," was all I could say.

"Fine with me," Death said with a shrug. "Ten years extension and your demise will not trigger the vamp's. We good?"

So very, very good. I bit my lip again to keep from crying with relief.

He offered a hand.

"Chloe," Killion growled. "You don't need to do this for me."

It *was* for him. For both of us. I slid my palm into

Death's. "One year of grim work in exchange for all that. I accept."

Pain pierced my skin as his magic sliced open the center of my palm. His own blood, filled with his death magic, mixed with mine. I smelled grave dirt, felt the billions of souls on the other side of the veil, my body racked with his power, my own rising to match it.

A sweet, yet painful, euphoria rushed through me. There was an edge I didn't remember from previous blood oaths with him. A metallic taste filled my mouth. Grim Zero sighed.

"Your new signed and sealed employment extension with your terms spelled out is in your inbox. Tinder will drop by tomorrow to put your thumbprint in the book." Our combined blood dripped onto the white linen table-cloth, pooling in a macabre image of a scythe. The smile Death gave me was all-consuming. "Welcome aboard for another year, Grave Girl."

TWELVE

I listened to Killion's rant on the way to the private cemetery where Pepper's grandmother had been buried. I deserved it and accepted his anger, knowing I'd done the right thing.

Ghost lay in my lap, her warm body a solid weight. She seemed more content than she had in days, as if she had sensed my upheaval of emotions over my employment contract and her fate. She probably had, and was now relieved. I was simply grateful she was back to normal and I had another year to figure out how to keep her indefinitely.

Corvus rode up front with Moss. When Killion finally fell silent, I took his hand in mind and wove my fingers between his. "You have every right to be upset, but I'm asking you to have faith in me." I stared into his eyes with purpose, pushing my magic at him. "There are things going on up here"—I tapped my temple and then pointed upward, signaling Death could be listening—"that I can't explain, but I know what I'm doing."

His beautiful violet eyes darkened, but he appeared to understand my message. "I see." He drew me to him, kissing the top of my head when I laid it on his shoulder. "Are you sure you're okay with this? Continuing to work for SMG?"

"I am." It wasn't exactly a lie. I'd do anything to protect him and Ghost. "Everything is going to work out for us. I know it is."

He stroked my hair. "I believe in you, you know. I may not like everything you do, or how you go about solving problems, but I've watched you overcome each challenge thrown at you in the past year. It's not simply your power that makes you a formidable supernatural. It is your emotions and the way you balance them with logic and strategy."

I dropped a light kiss on his cheek. "I believe in you, too."

"I must admit knowing that I have extra time with you fills me with joy."

That was an understatement for me. I was elated. "Ten years is still not enough, but think of what we can do in that time."

He squeezed me tight, and things might have gone further if we hadn't arrived in front of the small but carefully tended resting place of Pepper's ancestors.

She and Andy greeted us as we approached. Ghost ran ahead and sniffed at them, as well as Pepper's sister, but then paused at the entrance to the property, plunking her butt down and waiting.

I was proud of her and her show of reverence. I wanted to pick her up and hug her, but instead, I found myself embraced by Pepper, her sister standing a few feet behind us.

"We weren't sure you would show," the red-haired female said.

The cold press of ghosts raised gooseflesh under my suit. "Why wouldn't I?"

Pepper released me. "We know you have important matters to attend to." She worried a piece of leather fabric in her hands. "This isn't really your job."

"When the dead are disturbed, it *is* my job." I squeezed her arm. Such a complicated history between us, but my heart ached for her. "Plus, you're my friend."

Her face brightened but her bottom lip trembled. "I can't thank you enough."

She walked Killion and I to the entrance, the grave-yard laid out in an awkward triangle, the tip of which faced north. There were no fancy crypts here, the dead buried in the ground. Ghost stayed close and peeked up at me, patient and waiting. Centuries of old shifter magic coiled in the air like tendrils of mist and smelled of loyalty and deep family ties. There were plenty of lingering spirits here, but we weren't taking any to the other side tonight.

Pepper held out the leather. "I brought this. I wasn't sure if you needed something of hers to call her to you."

I typically didn't; ghosts just came. The material was soft under my fingertips. "She may have already crossed, you know."

Pepper gave a stoic nod. "I hope she has."

Her sister put an arm around her shoulders. "Is it

okay if we wait outside the perimeter? Looking at the grave...it's distressing."

"Wherever you're comfortable is fine." I cocked my chin at Andy. "Do you want him to remain with you?"

The woman shook her head. "I'm Farina, by the way. I'm sorry I bit you, you know, when you raised Andy. I wish we'd met under better circumstances."

"As do I. No other graves have been disturbed?"

Andy leaned on the low stone fence. "None. If the culprit returned, he or she must have sensed we were here and stayed away."

While they lingered, the three of us entered and I sent out a gentle pulse of my magic to alert the ghosts and offer an invitation. "I'm not here as a reaper," I called out. "I want to talk, if any of you are willing to help me identify those who have desecrated your sacred grounds."

I felt the presence of spirits drawing closer, but none materialized.

"You're sure it was ghouls?" Andy asked Killion under his breath.

The master vampire held his gaze. "Do you have an alternate theory?"

"If Trinity and her boy toy are trying to create a war between us, it's possible she wants us to believe a vampire did this."

Killion didn't miss a beat. "Vampires do not eat flesh."

"As you've pointed out, yet as I've pointed out, it's not a stretch from blood to a more substantial snack."

Killion's reaction roared through me with the force of a dozen tanks. "In case you are a moron and didn't realize it from our previous conversation, comparing us to ghouls is abhorrent."

Andy took a wise step back. "I'm just saying. The elder's body is a mess, and it's difficult to tell with any accuracy who or what tore it up. Even if a vamp didn't do it, whoever did may have made it look like it was one of your kind."

I stepped between them. "Let's save the theorizing for later. If I can get the elder, or any of the others here to speak to me, we'll learn who assaulted her and why."

"Show me the body," Killion demanded.

"It was taken to the morgue for cold storage until the sisters can arrange a new burial ceremony." Andy pointed to his left and a section cordoned off with yellow police tape. "The grave is there if you want to check it. I went over it thoroughly—none of the scent left behind smelled like ghoul."

"You know how they smell?" I asked.

"I do after scenting those three at Shepherd's Rest last night."

I touched Killion's arm, drawing his attention. "I'll get us into the morgue after we leave here."

He seemed appeased, but I felt the rage inside him caused by Andy's accusation.

"I give you my word," I called softly to the spirits present. I'd purposely left my scythe in the limo. Ghost sat at my feet. "I promise not to reap you, unless that's what you want. If you're tired of lingering on this plane, I can send you to the afterlife, which I assure you is quite nice. But if you prefer to be here, no problem. I won't touch you."

The gray, gauzy texture of the invisible world filtered over the area as I tuned into it. With my grave sight, I caught a few phantom figures hovering here and there, but whenever I looked at them straight on, they disappeared deeper into the invisible world. My assurances hadn't succeeded.

Rubbing the leather, I closed my eyes. "What was her name?" I asked Andy.

"Grandmother Yonah. Her ancestry is Cherokee. Her family was transplanted here from the Carolinas."

I silently repeated her name. "Your granddaughter is hurting, Grandmother, and seeks to right this wrong done to you. I'm a go-between who can give her a message. Tell me who did this."

The nearby nocturnal insects and frogs started their nightly chorus. I remained patient, calling her name over and over in my mind. If she had moved on, she might still feel my call and return long enough to answer questions. If this didn't work, we could try a seance. I'd alerted Aurora to be ready.

I was on my third round of repeating my request when ice slid over my shoulder, a finger of it traced down my spine. I held still, heart ratcheting up a notch. "I'm listening," I said softly, rubbing the material. "No harm will come to you. I only wish to help you rest easy, and bring peace to Pepper and Farina."

Tsgili, came a whisper. It echoed in my mind. *Tsgili, tsgili, tsgili.*

"Tsgili," I murmured. "Is that your attacker's name?"

"That's what they call a witch." Aurora emerged from the shadows of a spindly yew, crossing the chilled ground. She bowed to the wispy figure shape forming in front of me. The ghost nodded to the two of us, but didn't speak.

"I'm not a witch," I assured Yonah. "She is."

"We all have a little witch in us, don't we, Grandmother?" Aurora asked with a smile. To me, she added, "I believe she's referring to Trinity."

The figure shimmered, growing more translucent. I frowned. "Trinity did this?" A nod. "Not ghouls?"

A shake of her head.

"She made it appear as if they were involved to throw us off her trail," Killion murmured. He glanced Andy's way, acknowledging the shifter's idea wasn't completely ludicrous. "A clever distraction."

Outsmarted again. Or at least Trinity thought so.

Yonah's voice crawled through my mind, dry fall leaves skittering across the ground. *Spirit...bag.*

A thought clicked in my brain. "That's it."

"What?" Aurora asked.

"Thank you," I said to the ghost while motioning the others to head back. "Rest now. We'll return once we've worked this out."

She disappeared.

At the gate, Ghost rushed to Pepper and Farina. "Did you contact her?" Pepper asked. "Did you see her? Is she okay?"

"She was very helpful." I handed her the leather fabric. "Can you make her a new spirit bag?"

The sisters exchanged a glance. "I don't know," Pepper said.

"It's not something that's done," Farina added. "Each

is unique to its owner. Only they know what's in it and why."

"Use that fabric." I pointed to the piece. "Do your best to recreate one for her."

Another glance between them. Pepper frowned. "Why?"

"If my theory is correct, she's not going to want her previous one back."

Andy, Aurora, Killion and I climbed into the limo. Ghost laid in my lap, asleep before we pulled out.

"Did Trinity destroy the spirit bag?" Killion asked.

"In some ways," I said, before instructing Moss to head to the morgue. I still wanted to view the body, see if there was any type of mark on Yonah's remains.

"Oh no," Aurora said, catching on to what I'd concluded. "She didn't."

Andy and Killion scanned us in turn. "What?" Andy asked.

I fingered the sheath with my scythe tucked inside. *Kill*, the blade whispered to me. *Soon*, I whispered back. "She's turned the elder's spirit bag into her dark artifact."

THIRTEEN

Dwayne, the security guard, was at the front when we arrived. "Long time no see," he said, flipping through a magazine after barely glancing up. "Your uncle isn't here."

The morgue was situated in a separate annex from the hospital with an underground walkway linking them. It was a few hundred yards from the rear of the police station, and tonight, the desk was decorated with a single jar candle filling the place with the scent of pumpkin spice. On any given shift, hospital personnel, as well as cops, might visit or drop off bodies.

I had to play this right, since I was no longer an employee of the hospital morgue. "Ah, you know Uncle Morty, he's always late. I'm meeting him for dinner." I held up a foil covered container that Pennyworth had put together quickly for us when we'd made a pitstop at the penthouse after dropping Andy and Aurora off at her place.

Dwayne sat taller, his nose wriggling as he caught

scent of the fried chicken and mashed potatoes. "Did you make that? Smells delicious."

As planned, my cell rang at that precise moment. "Hey, Uncle Morty." I paused to listen as Killion, pretending to be my uncle, said he wasn't going to be able to have dinner with me. "That's okay." Pause, pause. "Don't worry about it. Another time, then."

I disconnected, looking sad. "Guess our date is postponed. Too bad since this food won't keep."

He licked his lips. "I'd be happy to take it off your hands."

"You're welcome to it." I placed it in front of him. "How are things around here?"

He snatched napkins from his drawer and tucked one into his collar before unveiling his unexpected dinner. "Quiet tonight. That new gal is working out pretty good, by the way."

I loitered, watching him dig into a chicken leg. "Glad to hear it. How is Mary Lynn?"

He licked his fingers, swallowing a large bite. "Seems normal." He helped himself to a portion of the mashed potatoes. "She's got a new girlfriend. Things are getting serious, too. I didn't know you were such a good cook."

I wished I could take credit for it. I checked my watch. How long would this take? "Actually, a friend made it, but he'll be thrilled to hear you enjoyed it."

"Really good," he said around a mouthful. He blinked. "How's that dog of yours?"

"Sassy as ever."

His movements slowed. He eyed my ring. "Heard you were getting..."

I snatched the dish back right before his head thunked into it, him succumbing to the sleeping potion I'd drugged the meal with. He wouldn't remember any of this when he woke. "Sorry, Dwayne," I murmured, patting a chubby jowl.

My skin tingled. Killion, invisible, swept past me. A moment later, the cameras blinked off and the door buzzed to let me in. The video footage of my interaction with Dwayne would be wiped, thanks to Killion's magic. I tossed the plate into the trash bin.

As I hustled through the entrance to the main area, my uncle's sign on the wall caught my attention.

We speak for the dead. Respect and honor them.

Stick to the facts, and do not suppose you know what their life was like.

In the end, we are all the same—none of us gets out of this world alive.

Killion and I hadn't been inside The Pit, as it was nicknamed, in a long while. The smell hit first, a combo of antiseptic and cleaning products overlaid with the candle's fragrance, bringing back memories as we scanned the metal doors stacked three high against the wall. "Any guess as to which one holds Yonah?" I asked.

Dressed in his usual suit and tie, the master vampire looked completely out of place, and yet, entirely at ease. He zeroed in on the last row, middle drawer. "This one."

Together, we opened it and slid the tray containing her out enough to examine. What was left was in a body bag and did not resemble a normal cadaver. I stopped Killion's hand before he unzipped it. "Wait." I offered a quiet prayer to honor her, my uncle's teachings well ingrained in me, even though I'd already spoken to her ghost.

Killion understood and held the silence with me, waiting until I gave him a nod before continuing.

I'd seen some upsetting sights in my time as the morgue's previous office manager, but this one, along with its odor, had me stepping back and gagging. Even Killion paused, his energy spiking at the gaping, torn flesh. He waved a hand over it to smoother the reek.

My gaze skated away to land on Uncle Morty's desk in the far corner. A row of plastic toy figurines from his favorite movies and television shows lined the back, his Wednesday Addams doll seeming to lock eyes with me. While my uncle respected the dead, he took himself lightly, always looking for ways to bring humor into the 'morbid' workplace. I recited the rules in my mind, remembering that no matter what, I was here to set things right for the elder.

In the recesses of my mind, I wondered what Uncle Morty would think about my supernatural role as a reaper. Thankfully, I hadn't been forced out of the magical closet yet.

Keeping my gaze on Wednesday, a favorite character from my childhood, I swallowed my emotions over Yonah's poor body and focused on the facts. "What do you think?"

"Whoever did it meant for it to be found and blame placed elsewhere. Ghouls do not typically leave evidence such as this."

"How could Trinity do it? Last I knew, she didn't have fangs or claws."

"Demons often take other forms."

"Ragriel did this?"

"Possibly." He drew in a breath through his nose. "Regardless of the fact Andy found no traces at the grave, I scent shifter, vampire, and ghoul on the remains." He gave a disgusted shake of his head. "This is tinder to Trinity's fire. She wants to confuse us. Send us in conflicting directions."

"Which is what she excels at, and I'm sick of it." I caught my erupting emotions before they could knock me off center. "The real issue is the spirit bag. If she's desecrated it by turning it into a dark artifact, we have to destroy it."

"If only it were that simple."

I zipped the body bag closed, choking down my revulsion. "Why isn't it?"

"The spirit bag is tied to her soul. If we destroy it..." He shrugged.

I gripped the edge of the tray, a newfound dread taking hold. "You're kidding, right?"

"We have to sever her spirit from the bag or she may end up in a place she doesn't want to be forever."

The hits kept coming and I had to regulate my breathing. This was bad, bad business. "Do you know how to do that?"

"Knowing how and having experience with such a thing are very different. My guess is Aurora might have the knowledge we need. I do not."

Crossing my mental fingers, I whispered another prayer and returned Yonah's remains to the cooler. "I'm not letting this poor woman suffer more than she already has."

On the way to Aurora's, we were both quiet, lost in our thoughts and each other's, our telepathic channel wide open.

"If this hadn't involved Trinity," Killion said, "Death would not be allowing you to help Pepper and her sister, you know."

While I'd insisted the disturbance of a burial fell in my wheelhouse, and it was true I had investigated grave robberies previously, they had been tied to a case. Unless SMG deemed it a problem, I didn't normally look into such things. That was for human law enforcement. "I would be helping her, anyway. What Trinity and Rag have done is just...*wrong* on so many levels."

"Mei would frown on your involvement."

"She frowns on anything outside the rules. And she should. SMG is a governing body and rules are what they do best. I'm me, and if someone I care about comes to me for help, I'm giving it to them."

"One of the many reasons I love you." He kissed my knuckles. "I've been thinking the same—that I find SMG's rules to be a hurdle at times. Many in the supernatural community need help with a variety of issues, including crimes against them and their loved ones, but they cannot turn to the mundane police."

"It's unfortunate."

"I believe my skills could help. I'm giving consideration to opening my own private investigation service. For magic-wielders only."

I squeezed his arm. "For real?"

A nod.

"*Tare!*" It was a Romanian term similar to 'cool' in English. I was currently learning some of the language from him. "Our community needs that."

He held my gaze with speculation evident in his. "Initially, it will require more of my time, you understand. I can give more duties to Harlow and Katarina, and perhaps bring on an astute partner to assist with my investment services, but..."

"Do it." I dropped a kiss on his mouth. "Whatever it takes. I'll help, if you need me."

A rare smile ghosted his lips. "You're good with this?"

"*Da.*" I kissed him more thoroughly. "I want what you want. I think it's the best idea you've had since I've known you—outside of seducing me."

This teased a grin from him. "*I* seduced *you*? That's not how I remember it."

"You're old. Your memory is faulty," I goaded. "All that smoldering and your pretty boy looks, how could I resist?"

He laughed. Actually laughed. "I do not, nor have I ever, smoldered."

"You keep telling yourself that, master." I nuzzled his neck. "I'm proud of you."

Seemingly uncomfortable with the praise, he cleared his throat. The sound rumbled inside me. "I was thinking the same about you earlier. I'm proud of you."

"For what?"

"You've handled so much over the past year with such grace. Your heart always leads the way."

Couldn't say I'd had much of a choice, but it was true.

I didn't adhere much to rules and regulations—I went with my gut and emotions. "Good thing it belongs to you."

"I know it does, yet I confess, hearing you affirm that brings me pleasure."

Was he still worried about the connection between me and Death? Unfortunately, it might always be in the back of our minds. "Do you have a name for your new PI service?"

"Not yet."

"Something fun to think about in the middle of all this."

"Yes, but I will wait to announce anything formal until after we've dealt with Trinity."

I fiddled with his cuff. "You'll still work for SMG when they need you?"

"If you okay it."

"You know I will."

We approached Evil Eye Burials, and Ghost barked, announcing our arrival. Killion helped me out. "Once we discuss our theory with Aurora, we'll head to Shepherd's Rest and recruit a few ghosts."

FOURTEEN

A half-wall of stones ran around Evil Eye Burials, along with a towering black iron gate, both of which kept the graveyard closed off from curiosity seekers and ghost tours.

Ancient oaks, mystical yews, and weeping willows sheltered rows of raised beds containing the dead, along with centuries-old crypts and mausoleums. Dozens of statues watched us, but not the usual kind. No mournful angels standing guard over the souls here. Instead, there were giant ravens, skeleton grims, and yes, evil eyes.

As per normal, a hazy mist clung to the property and a few ghosts added to the scary movie atmosphere. Some of it was part of the glamour my favorite witch had cast over the place; the rest was real. It had once been a place reserved for those practicing the occult or possessing magic in some form. Not only did its occupants not wish to be placed in Christian holy ground, some preferred to stay anonymous about their abilities, even in death.

A willow next to the towering mausoleum greeted us

with a long, rustling curtain of limbs that blanketed a side of the building and flowed down concrete steps leading to the door. Pillars decorated the front and gargoyle statues with open mouths glared at us from the roof. Ghost snarled at them, remembering her last encounter with the one in Shepherd's Rest, and I couldn't blame her.

I'd texted Aurora to let her know we were en route and that I meant to interview ghosts but wanted to get her opinion on something else first. I'd filled her in on everything up to that point that Killion and I had discussed concerning the elder and her bag. We entered the outer chamber, making our way past multiple crypts, and she greeted us at the interior door with a frown but welcomed us inside, resetting the wards once we'd passed.

Being behind these walls, under her wards, I relaxed fully for the first time in months. No one could eavesdrop on my thoughts here.

Her home was part atrium, part laboratory, and part library. Rows of shelved books lined the area. Skylights and a single wall of windows allowed moonlight in, giving the space a contented yet mysterious feel. Plants, goddess statues, candles in all colors of the rainbow, crystals, tarot decks, and other divinatory tools covered every available surface.

I'd come to think of this place as another of my home-away-from-home spots.

A fire crackled in the large brick hearth, but nothing bubbled in the giant purple cauldron hanging above it. Water trickled down a stone partition near the floor-to-ceiling window, and light from the dozens of candles around the room reflected in the pool below. As per normal, her work station in the center was covered with bottles, droppers, and copper bowls. An expensive microscope and multiple open books and texts added to the mad scientist vibe.

Ghost bounded toward her black cat stretched out in front of the hearth. She hissed and batted at the dog's muzzle in greeting and Ghost wagged her tail and started grooming the feline's fur.

Corvus croaked and flew to a swing connected to a tree branch growing from a live specimen near the waterfall. He danced on it for a moment, then settled, ruffling his wings and closing his eyes. My pets also felt like this was a home for them.

Aurora's hand hovered over a cup, warming the contents for me. She'd scooped her dark red curls into a tight bun on top of her head and wore a pair of sweats. "Ghosts are unreliable as sources." She shoved the cup at me, forgoing any small talk. "I hesitate to use them for covert operations."

Killion paced. "Agreed, and speaking of covert operations"—he eyed me—"can we discuss what happened at dinner?"

Sighing as the taste of mint hit my tongue and warmth spread through my body, I considered laughing, then crying with joy. I'd been holding my thoughts close, not allowing them to run free like usual for so long I wanted to skip around the room and shout hallelujah. I'd manipulated my thoughts, as well as my friends, into convincing Death I truly wanted to quit.

Which I still did in many ways. My arguments

weren't a lie—I wanted to devote myself to the clinic and spend as much time with Killion as possible before my soul contract expired and I returned to the great beyond.

Being able to think whatever I wanted, say whatever I wanted, inside this safe zone made me giddy. My new agreement was signed, sealed, and delivered, and nobody could accidentally give me away. Aurora's home was one of the only places I knew of that was protected by wards Death could not penetrate. "I had coaching from Grim Zero and it worked."

They stared at me, uncomprehending.

I sipped my beverage, not able to keep the grin off my face. "I needed everyone to believe I had no intention of extending my employment with SMG. I even had to convince myself. It was the only way to make sure Death believed it. If he discovered I was trying to manipulate the agreement, he would have the upper hand, and I wanted more than my five years."

"I don't understand," Aurora said. "What did you do?"

Killion's expression was stony, yet I saw his reluctant acknowledgment of my strategy. "She schemed to get Death to negotiate and extend her life."

My friend's face morphed with surprise and happiness. "How long?"

"Another ten past my remaining life."

She whooped and the cat jumped up and raced into her bedroom. Ghost followed, giving a playful bark, thinking it was a game. "That's fantastic. So you *do* want to stay on as a reaper? You sure had me fooled."

"I'm sorry about the deceit." The words were

directed as much at Killion as her. "Death has been eavesdropping on my mind. Not all the time, but Grim Zero knew it was happening, so I did as well. I couldn't risk him or SMG realizing they held the cards. I had to be convincing about refusing to continue as a grim in order to get them to agree to a new life term for me. While I could have come here and told you both under these wards, you would have had the information in your brains. I couldn't risk Death scanning you, too, and discovering it before I got him to negotiate with me."

"It was a clever ruse," Killion said. "Congratulations."

Aurora made a face at his dry, emotionless tone. "Why aren't you jumping for joy? You get more time together."

"I assure you I'm pleased where that is concerned." His fierce gaze said otherwise. "What I'm upset about is the part of the deal that relieves me from departing this world upon her death."

Aurora warmed another cup. "You're bound for eternity. If one dies, so does the other."

"Not in this case," I said, secretly gloating even though Killion was ticked. Death and Killion would never truly be friends and I'd played that card, knowing Death was jealous and splitting us up would make him happy. "It's a sealed deal with Death himself—when I die, it will not trigger Killion's demise."

Her brows hit her hairline. "You are a genius. A true master negotiator."

Killion folded his arms over his chest. "I will not walk this earth when you cease to."

"Here's the thing." I slid off the stool and faced him.

"In the event of my death at any point in time, including when I face Trinity in the next twenty-four hours, I need you to take care of Ghost, Corvus, even my aunt and uncle. You and Aurora. Make sure the pets are taken care of, my clinic continues on, and my family members don't suffer unnecessarily. Please."

"There's this thing called a last will and testament," Aurora said flippantly.

"I have one." Sort of. I touched Killion's arm. "In the aftermath of my croaking, be it now or down the reaper road, I want the assurance that you'll be here to handle things. Once you have, if you want to join me, so be it. I'll be waiting in the afterlife for you."

"You should have negotiated to keep Ghost once you're done reaping."

Of course, I'd wanted to. "If I'd asked for too much, he would have dug in his heels. I'd do anything to keep her, but I had to choose my battle moves wisely. You were the clear winner."

He stood unmoving, unblinking. It was almost as if he were seeing me for the first time and I couldn't discern what he had on in his mind. As the long silence made me twitchy, he said, "Very well."

He was still pissed. I got that. I would be the same in his shoes. "Thank you."

And then he grabbed me and yanked me into his arms, hugging me as fiercely as he'd just glared at me. "You continue to make everything hard."

He'd asked me once why everything with me had to be hard. I still had no answer. "I'm sorry I upset you, but I needed to do this. You're the only one, besides Aurora, who I trust and who knows me as the magical creature I am. I can't exactly bequeath Ghost to my aunt and uncle, and Death claims she'll be paired with another grim. If that happens, I want you to be sure it's a good one and they understand her quirks. These areas of my life need special handling."

No one said anything. Killion's energy relaxed. He rubbed my back. "I do not like it, and I will not tolerate further negotiations that we do not discuss ahead of time, but I do understand."

I smiled into his chest. "Fair enough."

"You two are adorable," Aurora said.

Killion growled low in his throat and I broke free of his hold, turning to address her. "We have a potential problem."

She grinned. "Only one?"

Touché. "We need your advice."

"We have a witch working with a demon hybrid to bring Armageddon on us. What's more problematic than that?"

I took my seat at her worktable. "If we obliterate the dark artifact, which was created with Yonah's spirit bag, will it endanger the elder's soul?"

"You know as well as I do that a soul cannot be destroyed."

"But they can be damaged, right? Left in a type of purgatory or hell?"

She set down her mug. "Stuck in torment? Yes. That in-between space that you can cross? It holds a lot of crea- tures, and some are trapped souls. They can't return here, but they can't move on, either."

"How do we separate Trinity's dark magic from the artifact so we don't do that to Yonah?"

Her lips pursed and she eyed one of her bookshelves. "I'm not sure you can. I'll have to do some research."

I tried to lighten the moment. "Can I get on Wiki How and look it up? We're kind of tight on time."

Her glare could cut ice. While she used the internet on occasion, she called most witchy sites "neo-pagan garbage."

"Just kidding," I said. *A little*. I actually used the site on a frequent basis and found it extremely helpful.

"We *are* running short on time," Killion said. "Can we help you?"

She crossed the room, reaching here and there to retrieve volumes until her arms were full. Returning, the books made a loud *thump* as she dropped them onto the tabletop. She handed several to me, then him. "Breaking black magic spells is not for the faint of heart and can go horribly wrong if done incorrectly. When it comes to one that's tied to a soul? That's even more advanced. We can't simply splinter or fracture the curse, we have to banish all traces of evil and Trinity's magic from the spirit bag and purge it. I've seen it done; it's...intense, and so much can go wrong. Then we'll have to hope we can restore Yonah's rightful energy to it."

"Intense, great." I accepted the books. "But if you've seen it done, then it *is* possible."

"It was a unique situation and called for extreme spellwork." She led us to her version of a living room and Killion and I sat on her couch, while she took an uphol-stered chair. "We have to do a Soul Rebirth spell. It's a three-step process, and I've never done it before." She tapped the cover of one of her books. "That's what we're looking for."

"What about talking to the ghosts?" I asked Killion. "Should we do that first?"

He checked his watch. "Let's wait until after midnight."

As we each read, various facts kept pushing to the front of my mind. "Trinity has misled us every step of the way, Ragriel helping her. That initial night I spoke to her in Shepherd's Rest, it was like she wasn't all there. The way she disappeared...he did the same thing. He seemed to materialize out of nowhere, then vanished in a puff of smoke. Last night, he sort of shimmered, and I didn't sense him until he walked right up on us. Is it possible the two of them are using bilocation?"

Aurora looked up from her open volume. "My spells all point to that cemetery."

Killion paused in his skimming. "Could she cloak their physical bodies and your divination tools are picking up on their projections instead?"

Her brows squeezed. "Yes. It's clever. Very, very clever."

"Remember," I reminded them, "she's playing with a being who is both angel and demon. Death pops in and out as easy as snapping his fingers. Rag could be the one causing the projections or screwing with your spells to keep us off kilter."

Her frown deepened. "But then where are their physical bodies? The dark artifact had to be in the church when we saw that thunderstorm display. Is it possible they're beneath the foundation?"

"Katarina checked the church and found nothing."

I glanced at Killion. "But they could be hiding under it. Something for us to investigate."

He took out his cell. "We'll let Harlow and Katarina do that." At Aurora's cocked brow, he explained. "Death and I believe that Trinity may need Chloe's blood to complete her destruction of the veil."

"Because you're the vortex," Aurora said to me.

Killion nodded. "It's imperative they do not capture her."

She shot a glance to me. "I already told you that."

"Yeah, yeah, you're both right. I'll stay away from them, okay?" I sank deeper into the sofa, closing the book I was holding and rubbing my eyes. "Since Rag is part angel, is there any way to pull him back into the light and make him good once more?"

"That would be a question for Death," Aurora said.

I wasn't in the mood to spar with him again so soon, so I dropped it and returned to searching for anything that would help us in our fight.

"I may have something," Killion said, glancing at us and tapping the open page in his lap.

Aurora smiled. "I do, too."

Now we were getting somewhere.

By the time we left, Killion and I each wore amulets to protect ourselves against Trinity's magic, and Aurora had drawn sigils on our chests in ceremonial ink charged with protection. We hoped it would work against Rag, too, but since Aurora couldn't be a hundred percent positive of her magic against that of a hybrid like him, it was best to avoid him. He'd been particularly aggressive at our last encounter.

All I wanted to do was speak to a couple ghosts and then we'd pull back. For Killion's plan and Aurora's magic to work, we'd need to make sure neither of our targets suspected what we were up to.

As we sped through the night on our way to Shepherd's Rest, I prayed I'd be able to pull off one more covert operation.

FIFTEEN

Wouldn't you know, when I needed a ghost, I couldn't find one.

Killion, Aurora, and I circled the perimeter of Shepherd's Rest once, me calling any earthbound spirits to appear and promising them, as I had Yonah, that I would not send them packing to the other side. While the dead in their graves itched to come to me, the spirits who normally haunted the place thumbed a nose at my assurance.

"This is getting us nowhere," I groused, fingering the silver amulet at my neck.

"You've sent dozens of their kind to the other side," Aurora reminded me. "You can't blame them for avoiding you since they prefer staying."

"The recent activity here may have scared them off as well," Killion murmured. "Or Trinity may have realized they could spy on her and she's quarantined them."

I liked her less and less. I hopped onto a flat crypt and picked at my nails. An encounter with the Fae came to mind and gave me an idea. "I'll owe you a favor," I called into the night. "All I need you to do is tell me where to find the dark witch, Trinity, or her demon master."

"What kind of favor?" a trembling voice asked behind my right shoulder.

Finally. "Anything within the realm of what I can do for you. What do you need?"

The apparition was grainy and she wore a long, prairie style dress, suggesting she'd been here a long time. "Revenge."

Not surprising. "For what?"

She grimaced, showing bad teeth. "What do you think?"

"Did someone take your life?"

Her dark eyes jumped to Killion and back to me. "My husband."

I scanned her getup. "And he's still alive?"

This seemed to confuse her. "Course he is. Why would I be talking to y'all if he weren't?"

Spirits lost track of time, and often experienced mental slips concerning family and friends. "Give me his name and I'll look into it."

"Curtis Beecham."

"And you are?"

"Dottie Mae Duvall." She hovered a few feet off the ground, keeping herself outside arm's reach. "Kill him slow. He deserves it."

"I'm not killing anyone, Dottie May. I will, however, make sure he's brought to justice."

She spit at the ground. "Justice? What kind can there be for me? I'm already dead."

"I understand how you must feel, but sometimes there is no justice here on earth. If you go to the other side, however, you'll understand karma, and you'll not care nearly as much about what's going on here on this plane."

"What are you talking about?" She screwed up her nose and looked down at me. "It's an eye for an eye."

"You believe in heaven?"

Her suspicion grew. "What's that got to do with this?"

"There's no going back and fixing what he did to you, but you can move on and find peace. Leave justice and revenge to the Big Guy, and quit torturing yourself by refusing to enter the afterlife and be happy."

"You telling me what to do, child?"

This wasn't going the way I had hoped. "Believe it to not, I do have insight into how nice the afterlife is, in case you change your mind. For now, I'll find Curtis and let him know you wish him dead. Fair enough?"

Surprisingly, this seemed to appease her. "Witches are in league with the devil. I stay far away from the one who lives here."

"Trinity lives here? Where exactly?"

"She is a right evil one. Acts as if she owns this place. Where else would someone like her settle?" She motioned with her head toward the large mausoleum we'd staked out last night.

"There?" I glanced at Killion. *Was Trinity right underneath us the whole time?* "Are you sure?"

"I saw what you two were doing up there," she

chided, pointing at the roof. "Have you no shame? You're as wicked as she is."

"Not even close," I grumbled.

"Is she living underground?" Killion asked.

The spirit sneered at him, then jerked around to peer past her shoulder into the shadows. "What have you done, vampire?"

Killion frowned, then stepped toward me as an odd slithering energy flowed over us. The temperature dropped at least ten degrees.

Aurora stuttered, teeth chattering. "What is...th...th...that?"

I'd had ghosts pass through me and this was a similar sensation, as if pure ice coated my blood and bones. My grim tattoo came to life—the only warm spot on my body—as did Aurora's bespelled pendant. The crystal sent out a silver bubble of protective energy around me and Ghost. Killion and Aurora's did the same for each of them. Ghost shuddered as if she was going to shift, but Killion held out a hand to signal her not to. I was both surprised and not that she obeyed.

"Lord Reveux," a deep female, very Southern voice, dripped with equal parts politeness and sexuality. "How lovely to see you again."

The ghost vanished with a terrified yelp. The trees seemed to tremble and the dead in their graves woke with startling swiftness. The vision that appeared a few yards from us looked remarkably harmless, yet I, too, wanted to tremble.

The female entity was made of shadows and bone. Her skin glowed as pale as the moon overhead and her skirt, the color of blood and split up to her thigh, flowed in waves around her as she strolled our way. Thick, dark tresses in old fashioned curls draped her bare shoulders. Flanked by phantoms on each side, she smiled warmly at Killion. After a deep inhale, her full lips parted on a sigh. "I love the smell of the dead, don't you?"

The phantoms snarled and growled, straining against invisible collars. If she released them, I feared our protective bubbles would be ripped to shreds.

"Revenants," Aurora whispered.

The being strolled closer, flicking her gaze over me before eyeing Killion as if he was a steak and she was a very hungry lion. "Your girl is pretty."

"Girl?" I bit out. "Are you talking about me?"

Killion slid in front of me like a shield and touched my hand in warning. Ghost planted her tiny feet next to him, baring her teeth. "Aveena. It has been a while."

"Miss me?" she cooed.

"What is *she*...do...doing...here?" Aurora ground out through her chattering teeth.

The thing that resembled a woman turned her attention on the witch and every hair on my body stood at rigid attention. Magic, old and corrupt, teased around our bubbles, seeking a crack to slip inside. "Gossip abounds." Her almond shaped eyes slid to Killion again. "My pets tell me you have been accusing my children of crossing into your territory and violating graves."

I started to step out of his shadow but his magic clamped down on me like a straitjacket. "There are at least three in town. I've seen them myself. An elder's body was desecrated and the evidence left behind points to your ghouls."

The ghoul queen. Now it made sense.

Her lips formed a ruby pout. "We have an agreement. I have not encroached on your region and neither have my children. "

I dragged Aurora closer, pulling her into line behind Killion. He appeared unruffled, although I could feel his energy coiled and ready to strike. He made a sound of disbelief. "Are you aiding the demon and his witch?"

Her face scrunched. "Demon? Witch? Your affairs do not involve me. I know nothing about—"

Vampires and shifters emerged as one from the shadows, Aveena's words dying on her lips. There had to be a hundred or more, and they formed a wall inside the hedgerow.

Andy flicked his gaze to Aurora and shifted with a pop into his giant wolf form. The others followed suit becoming a range of animals, while the vampires displayed fangs, murderous intent in their glowing red eyes. Harlow, Katarina, Moss, and even Mason, were present.

Aurora tugged her hand from mine, her eyes going a bright blue.

Uh oh.

Sure enough, my friend transfigured into a panther with a forceful shudder. Ghost followed suit and transformed as well.

"Um, everybody take a deep breath," I said, exuding calm I didn't feel. "Let's talk this through."

Trust me, came Killion's voice in my head. "Now that

you're here," he said to the ghoul queen, "we can use your help in defeating our mutual enemy."

The revenants gnashed their teeth, hounds chomping at the bit. "Help you?" Her sloe eyes went left then right, assessing her odds of getting out of the graveyard alive. "When this is how you treat me?"

The way the vamps and shifters stood in solidarity to threaten her without making any further moves was impressive. I had no idea how powerful she was, but I had no desire to find out either. From the magic radiating off her, it was equal to Killion's. Maybe mine as well.

But all of us?

Trust me. Was this Killion's plan?

"Trinity and her master, a hybrid called Ragriel, plan to bring down the veil on Samhain. You can imagine what will happen if they do." Killion regarded her with a razor cold smile. "You're going to join us and see that such an event does not occur."

"Join you?" Her laugher was ice picks raking my spine. "Why would I do that? This is not my fight."

She started to turn and Andy snarled, backing up her and her pets.

"Your daughter is buried in St. Anne's cemetery," Killion said with steel in his voice.

Everyone fell silent.

I wasn't sure how it was possible for her face to become even paler, but she did. Fearsome, raging magic, sprayed from her hands and hit our bubbles. They did not shred, but they shook as if a tsunami had struck us. "What," she snarled, "have you done?"

I gripped Killion's arm. *What* have *you done?* I questioned.

"She's alive," he said, "and will remain so as long as you side with us in this war."

"I do not take sides," Aveena growled. "You know this."

"To sit back and do nothing is to do exactly that." His body was relaxed; suggesting confidence. He knew he had her. "Declare loyalty to me or she dies a long, slow, painful death."

Her eyes went wide, then narrowed. "She *is* one of you, or have you forgotten?"

The ghoul queen's daughter was also a vampire? My head spun.

"She is her mother's daughter," Killion replied. "Her life is in your hands."

"If she is harmed, you will *pay*."

I knew Killion on a soul level. Much of his past was a mystery to me, but he was fair and honest, if also cunning and exceptionally powerful. "If she is harmed," I spoke up, "it will be on your conscience, not his."

"Hush, child," she seethed. "You know not what you speak of."

"*Child?*" I stepped from behind Killion and glared at her. "You are so not getting a Christmas card from us this year. I'm Chloe Frost, aka Grim Zero. I'm sure you've heard about me through your gossip grapevine."

"Death's handmaiden." She flicked her gaze over me as if I were no more significant than a flea. "Someone should school you on proper manners."

I wanted to behead her there and then. I glanced at

her snarling pets, letting the clear threat of taking them out instead show in my eyes. "You're surrounded by the Undead and Shifter Nations and your daughter is buried alive. Or Undead-alive." Whatever. "As queen of the ghouls, you must be fairly intelligent. Can you not see that you're outnumbered and you've been outmaneuvered? Besides the fact that if this witch and demon succeed at tearing down the veil holding our worlds apart, you and your daughter will perish with the rest of us. Lose-lose."

Her irises glowed orange. "No entity can bring down the wall between worlds. Whatever game you're playing, I won't be part of it."

I wondered if Trinity and Rag were nearby listening. I didn't care if they were. "When the rest of us save this world—and we will—I'll be sure to harvest you and yours with swift, tactical precision."

Her eye twitched. "You can't do that if our contracts aren't up."

"I looked it up in my Grim manual," I lied. I hadn't opened the tomb in months. "Ghouls cheat death by using the bodies of the dead to remain alive past their expiration dates. My boss frowns on that kind of thing and Section 12A of my manual states, '*those who disturb the dead in any way to profit off them or control their spirits, whether on this plane or any other, are considered expendable by any means necessary.*'"

Section 12A had no such language, but rather had to do with a grim refusing to reap an assigned soul. She didn't know that, however, and her brow creased, her full lips pursing in thought once more. "Why has SMG not sent reapers after me and mine then?"

"You're low on the totem pole of their concerns. You stay in the shadows, keep a low profile, they leave you alone. But I have a mission to reap this witch. Your refusal to assist me constitutes obstruction of my duties." I gave her my nastiest smile. "You're now at the top of *my* list, right behind Trinity. I can call Death and request he join us if you'd like confirmation."

No one moved. Didn't so much as breathe. You could have heard a leaf break free from its branch and float to the ground.

My bluff paid off. While I saw the wheels turning, her too-long pause caused the others to become agitated. Low growls and grunts echoed around the circle. Corvus called from one of the trees. Drool dripped from Ghost's bared fangs onto my boots.

Andy lifted his head and howled, raising goosebumps on my skin. Others like him joined in, the sound deafening in the space.

Aurora scratched a massive paw in the lawn, her sharp claws leaving rivulets of torn grass in their wake. The noise that came out of her throat was half hiss, half snarl.

While Killion did not become his beast, most of his nest, including Harlow and Katarina, went full vamp. Even mild-mannered, sweet Mason showed a side I'd never witnessed before—and hoped I never saw again.

Aveena's seething pets stayed utterly still, but like any animal backed into a corner, seemed more dangerous, their eyes alight with the same orange glow as their master.

My palm heated, letting me know the blade was also ready to join the fray. I drew it from the sheath, slow and steady, not wanting to incite a riot but making sure the ghoul queen saw I meant business. "What will it be?"

The orange irises went red. Her lips curled away from her teeth and she took a step closer to Killion.

I gripped the scythe's handle tighter, expecting her to attack. *Kill*, the blade sang to me.

Do not, Killion commanded in my head.

Me: *But—*

Killion: *Trust me.*

I clenched my teeth and held my breath.

Aveena's skirts swished as she bent a knee in front of him, lowering herself to the ground and bowing her head. "I declare my loyalty to Lord Reveux for the next twenty-four hours." Her voice rang out clear, if not pleased. "Only to assist in the reaper's mission to harvest the witch. Once completed, this agreement between us expires." Her head rose and she glared at him through the bubble.

He gave her an appeased nod, then extended a hand to help her rise. The bubble vanished and she accepted his aid. "Welcome to my fold," he said, but there was nothing hospitable in his tone. Every word was laced with unspoken malice. "Here's what I require of you."

SIXTEEN

I paced the penthouse floor, so filled with anxiety, I could barely breathe. Sunrise—Halloween—was only a few hours away.

Killion and his nest were meeting at St. Anne's to go over his plan. The shifters and ghouls were joining them at sundown.

I battled my annoyance at being kept from the church, but he was right—he had the army he needed. I would not risk all of them because of my stubbornness to be part of the battle.

My job was to work with Aurora on the spell to separate Yonah's soul from her spirit bag when the time came.

"Do you need a sedative?" Pennyworth asked with total sincerity. "Perhaps some ice cream?"

Aurora, chanting over a pot of simmering herbs that made the place stink, snorted. She was lucky to have commandeered the kitchen from him, and he hovered at her elbows, frustrated that he couldn't help either of us.

"I'm too worried to eat."

The witch snorted again. "I've never known you to be unable to stuff your face."

She was as worried as I was, although she was hiding it better. Having something to do probably helped.

I screwed up my nose. "How much longer do you have to cook that?"

"Another few minutes. Everything has to be blended just so."

Pennyworth examined the various bottles on the island. "Salt, hyssop, basil, mug wort, patchouli, vetiver, wormwood. That's quite a recipe."

"Let's hope it works," she said, stirring three times clockwise, and then three in reverse while speaking softly in her witch language.

"It has to. We have to disconnect Yonah's soul before everything goes down."

"The timing will be a challenge, won't it?" Pennyworth inquired. He was beginning to show signs of nerves as well.

I worried my fingers and started pacing again. "First, they have to trap Trinity and Ragriel, then separate them from the spirit bag. Once they have that, Aurora has to work her magic on it before she and Killion destroy it."

"And then," she added, eyeballing a spoonful of the brew, "we have to figure out how to contain Ragriel before Chloe harvests Trinity."

Pennyworth shook his head. "I may be the one who needs that ice cream."

I patted his arm, trying to muster assurance. "Your

master has a plan. He's good at this. We'll pull it off, I promise. If it would make you feel better, you can go to your place. See Omwee."

His partner was sure to calm him, but the butler shook his head. "We have tasks to do for the master."

A knock sounded and the three of us shared a guarded look. At the same time, Pennyworth's face relaxed, his vampire telepathy tapped into the hotel staff. One of them must have told him who it was. "There's a young gentleman from SMG here."

He left the kitchen as I puzzled out who that might be. I followed. "Not Death?"

"No." He opened the door. "I assume you're here for Ms. Frost."

Tinder, Mei Han's messenger and contract manager, lifted the beefy book he typically carried and gave me the once over. Six feet and angular, he wore a newspaper boy hat cocked sideways on his head and a wool jacket the color of my raven. His eyes darted around over my head, as if searching for Killion, and he toyed with the frayed leather straps holding the beefy volume closed. "Boss is on my tail about getting your paperwork in."

Of course she was. Type A did not begin to cover Mei's fixation with details. "I'm a little busy."

Before Pennyworth could allow him in, the elevator dinged, and a woman the size of an eight year old and dressed to the nines strode out. A giant, hulking vampire with a hump between his shoulder blades trailed after her, bolts of fabrics in his arms. She glanced up at us from under a hat with a veil, her face that of a forty-something femme fatale even though she was well under five feet, before she pulled up short. "Where is my client?"

Tinder took a step back, raising his empty hand. "Not me."

She huffed and spoke to Pennyworth. "Well?"

Always the epitome of adeptness and grace, he swept an arm out, motioning her inside. "Right this way, Estrid."

Her assistant had to duck to enter. He loped past me and went to the dining room table, dropping his load there.

"What's going on?" I asked.

"Estrid, this is Chloe Frost, the master's intended." Pennyworth turned to me. "Chloe, Estrid, the seamstress."

She plucked at my t-shirt. "Perhaps we should start with a wardrobe adjustment before we tackle a dress fit for the Master's bride."

Tinder, sliding in behind her, snickered.

I whirled on the butler. "We're doing this *now*?"

"Estrid has a full schedule, and since the master insisted you stay here..." He gave a slight shrug. "I thought it prudent to multitask."

The female vamp sniffed. "My time is valuable, Ms. Frost, and your request tests the boundaries of what I'm capable of accomplishing in such a short peri-od." It was odd to hear a commanding, adult voice coming from such a small person. "I can fit you in now, or you may feel free to have someone else create your gown."

Aurora peeked her head out to see what was going on. She scanned the dining room and the sour looking

Lurch figure standing at the table. "I'll be in here, unless you need me." She disappeared back into the kitchen.

There honestly wasn't much for me to do, so reluctantly, I motioned at the bolts of fabric. "Do I need to pick one of these?"

Tinder glanced at his steampunk watch. "I'm on deadline, too, y'know."

Exasperated, I held out my thumb. "Do it."

He set the book on the coffee table and it magically opened to a tea-stained page. My last entry glowed and a new column formed on the paper with the heading, *2nd Year*. Grabbing my thumb, he slammed the end onto the correct line and I felt a prick. My grim tattoo spiked hot and sizzled, and I bit my bottom lip. Although I was prepared this time, it was still painful.

"Right, then." He slammed it shut and tucked it under his arm. "Good doing business with you, Grim 281. I'll show myself out."

When he got to the door, he turned back and caught me sucking my thumb. "I heard about what's going down later. Keep your wits about you, eh?"

I grinned. "That sounds suspiciously like you care about me."

He rolled his eyes and scooted across the threshold. "A replacement means more paperwork and a big headache for me, that's all."

Before closing the door, however, he winked. Then he was gone.

Estrid had already marched into the other room and withdrew a sketchpad from her messenger bag. She flipped through pages and pages of elaborate drawings and began showing me the gowns she had designed. "With your figure, this would be my choice."

It was a flamboyant thing with a high neck, long sleeves, and a skirt that flared out at the bottom. The bodice was embroidered with gold tassels and lined with matching buttons. More detailed embroidery flowed over the hips and down the skirt. Even as a simple drawing, everything about it screamed "royalty."

I swallowed, the realization of what I was about to commit to hitting home and making my limbs shaky. My vision blurred and I blinked hot tears away, unsure if they were caused by being overwhelmed or fear. "That's stunning."

Pennyworth peered over my shoulder and clapped his hands. "It's perfect! We'll put your hair up in loose curls. Some heirloom earrings and—"

"Um...yeah," I stammered, interrupting. I wasn't a traditional modern bride, to be sure. Neither was I a traditional vampire one. "This is fit for a queen. It's just not right for me."

The seamstress gave me a condescending once over. "Perhaps then you need an upgrade."

I counted to five so as not to lash out and reached for Killion-level composure. I threw in a trace of don't-mess-with-me Chloe-ness, for good measure. "What I need is an elegant gown to marry Lord Reveux," I said. "In case anyone has forgotten, *I* am the one who is bonded to him for eternity."

She drew back, the meaning of my words sinking in. He wasn't only her master, he was my everything and I was his. He cherished me above all others, and while I had no intention of lording my status over them, I wasn't going to put up with being bullied into what someone else wanted. It was our ceremony, and I had a say in what I wore.

That settled, I grabbed the pad and began searching through the designs. "Nothing ostentatious. I want to honor his ancestry and the importance of this ceremony, but I also want something that feels good and moves when I do." One in particular caught my eye. "I like this." I turned the pad around to show it to her.

Pennyworth moved to view it and even Lurch leaned over to check it out.

A stiff silence filled the air, then Estrid said, "A lovely choice." Her words didn't match her stiff, offended posture, but this was progress nonetheless. "May I make a suggestion?"

"Absolutely."

"An open, scooped neckline would be more elegant than the halter top."

I stared at the sketch, the style reminding me of my mother. She'd loved halter tops, but I had nice shoulders and Killion loved my collarbone and, go figure, my neck. "I'm open to the idea. Get it?" I smiled. "Open?"

Her face reflected the fact she found my pun beneath her. With quick fingers, she snagged a pencil from the top of her ear and quickly sketched a new design. She fingered a bolt of rich purple satin and nodded. "This is soft and will melt over your curves. The color suits your skin tone and we could add contrasting insets in the skirt with this shade." She unwrapped a length of plum, draping it over the other, and deftly amended the gown taking shape on paper. "They will flare open when you walk and the sheen of the satin will reflect the light."

My mind flashed to an image of me walking down the aisle on Uncle Morty's arm, Killion waiting at the end. I saw him smile, his eyes running over me and the gown, and felt his total enchantment. "I love that idea."

Over the next few minutes, she would motion at her assistant, who seemed to read her mind, and he would bring varying trims, buttons, and intricate laces to lay beside the chosen fabrics.

I rolled a length of piping with faceted smoky crystals between my fingers. "These are beautiful. I love how they flash."

She grabbed her pencil once more from its spot over her ear and added a border of them along the illustrated neckline. "We'll also add a row at the end of each sleeve."

By the time Aurora announced the potion was done, Estrid was returning her pad to the messenger bag and her assistant was cramming his arms full of the bolts once more. "I'll have the sample ready for you next week," she said in her no-nonsense voice. "Would you prefer for me to bring it here for the fitting, or would you rather visit my shop so it remains a secret from the master?"

I hated secrets, but in this case, it made me smile. I would have to blank my mind and close our channel so he didn't get a peek before our wedding day, but it would be worth it to see that look on his face. "If I'm still alive, and the world is not overrun by monsters, I'll come to your place." At her nod, her assistant drew out a cell to schedule an appointment on her calendar. He glanced at me in question and I knew he wanted a date and time. "I'll make it at your convenience," I said to the seamstress.

While her icy expression flickered with a faint smile, she remained as stiff and unfriendly as before. I knew I'd scored points, though, when she said, "Call me when you have a free moment and we will discuss a time beneficial to both of us."

The two of them headed for the door, and Pennyworth rushed to open it. She paused and scanned me from head to toe again. I assumed she was going to make a comment about my clothing choice. "I will see you next week. Your mission tonight will be successful."

Stunned, I eyed her more carefully. "Are you psychic?"

This invoked another muted smile, then she strode for the elevator. Her assistant hesitated and whispered over his shoulder to me, "She believes in positive thinking."

Vampires never failed to surprise me.

Pennyworth closed the door and looked like a kid on his birthday. "That gown is going to be gorgeous. It will knock the master's socks off, as humans say."

"I'm excited about it." And I was. Thinking about the ceremony was a bit less terrifying now. I wondered why picking a dress, of all things, had caused me so much distress. "I think I put it off so long because I've been afraid to disappoint him. On the other hand, I have to be me."

He waved away my words. "You could never disappoint him, and I think what you did for him last night concerning your employment with SMG was very brave.

I, for one, appreciate it, and I know the other Undead do, as well. You've earned their respect, you know."

I hadn't, but hearing it now buoyed my spirits.

Aurora had snuck in behind us. "Well," she said, holding up a bottle of liquid and eyeing it, "let's hope we don't test that addendum tonight."

SEVENTEEN

Killion, Andy, and Katarina returned before sundown.

Along with Aurora, we gathered in Killion's office, his massive desk cleared of its usual accruements to make room for a strategy board and map of Danté's Grove. He used figurines from his favorite chess set to represent the different parties.

"The ghost tours will be in full swing until midnight," he said. "Trick-or-treaters will be out, and plenty of adults will be partying as well. As of two this afternoon, I created the illusion of sinkholes at both entrances of Shepherd's Rest and the city has declared the place a hazard so it is off limits to the general population."

Katarina positioned three of the figurines on the map. "We currently have patrols watching for errant kids or ghost hunters seeking entry anyway. They will be compelled to move on."

"Smart," Aurora said.

Andy beamed. "It was my idea."

Katarina rolled her eyes.

"Won't Trinity notice," I asked, "and assume we're planning an attack?"

"Yes," Killion confirmed, "but we will use that to our advantage. She'll believe we have brought the sacrificial goat to the party, and we'll give her a dose of her own medicine in the tricks department."

"Wait, what?" I said. "You told me I couldn't go."

He held up a finger. "I'll circle back to that." Using other chess pieces, he placed them in strategic areas on the map as he spoke. "My team will be in charge of separating the hybrid from the witch and removing him to St. Anne's." He pointed at Andy. "Yours will keep her entrapped at Shepherd's Rest. While Aurora inspects and dismantles the dark artifact, Death will arrive with his squad from SMG and remove Ragriel to a safe location where he will be imprisoned. When we are sure the artifact no longer holds power, I will bring Trinity to St. Anne's where the real Chloe will harvest her."

It sounded simple and straightforward, yet was the farthest thing from it. I felt like I was missing a piece of the overall puzzle. "How do you plan to control Ragriel while detaching him from Trinity?"

Aurora tapped the side of her neck. "Remember the mark I told you about? I believe if I can disfigure it, their symbiosis will take a hit. Ragriel should have a matching one, and when Killion traps him—"

Katarina rubbed her hands together. "I'll rip his right off him."

Aurora frowned but nodded. "By marring both, it

should weaken the cord between them, if not sever it entirely."

"How are you getting close enough to Trinity to do that?" I asked.

Killion was always serious, but tonight even more so. "That's what I'm circling back to. We have a stand-in for you. She will act as you, and in the process, get close enough to Trinity to mutilate the mark."

Remind me to never get on your bad side. I shook my head. "I don't understand. How can someone stand in for me? Trinity has seen me."

Aurora jiggled the bottle of potion. "I'm going to become you, confusing her. I'll allow her to capture me, and at the right moment, I'll strike."

I had so many questions, I didn't know where to start. "You're going to pretend to be me? You don't look anything like me. Even with a wig and low lighting, she won't be fooled."

"I'm good at transfiguration, remember?" She patted my arm. "Normally, you wouldn't be my first choice to impersonate, no offense, but in this case, I'll make an exception."

"None taken," I replied automatically. "You can actually do that?" I pointed at the bottle. "I thought that was for the spirit bag."

"Oh, I have one for that, too. This is to help me become you, at least, as far as looks go."

My Harry Potter fangirl kicked in once again. "You mean like Polyjuice Potion?"

"That's one way to think of it."

I eyed the liquid, unable to keep from making a face. "Does it hurt?"

"Since I'm not a shifter by nature, any reshaping of bones doesn't exactly feel good, but it will be worth it."

So devious, I telegraphed to Killion. *You're brilliant.*

He offered a wicked, confident smile.

To my friend, I said, "I bet it tastes bad."

The witch laughed, knowing how much I despised her teas. "Not everything in life is sweet, Chloe."

"And not everything is as dangerous as this," I reminded all of them. "What if something goes wrong? Trinity could kill Aurora. I'm not sure I am okay with this plan."

"Neither am I," said Andy, "but I was outvoted, and I can assure you that you will be, too."

Aurora's face went hard, her green eyes flashing. "Trinity is not any more powerful of a witch than I am, she simply has an extra battery to juice her spells. I know what I'm doing."

"Aurora is as experienced, and as powerful as, Trinity," Killion said, earning a look of approval from her. "The ploy is sound and is our best gambit to maneuver Trinity into our trap."

"She's tricky," Katarina said, "but so are we. We'll flip the script on her."

Aurora needed no one to validate her magical abilities, yet her chin stayed lifted over Killion's complimentary words. "I volunteered for this assignment and I will accomplish what needs to be done."

Andy and I exchanged a glance of support, knowing it was a moot point to argue.

"We must not allow Trinity to gain control of Aurora too easily." Killion studied his arrangement of figurines. "Nothing about our movements must give away our true strategy or make Trinity suspicious and change hers."

"I've been going over different variations of capturing her," Andy said. "My team will be ready for anything she tries, and I will be there to protect Aurora."

He said the last sentence with emphasis, locking eyes with her.

She glanced down, her lips pressing together, but I felt her appreciation of his fealty. I reached over and clasped her hand. "That you would do this for me means everything."

Her eyes rose to meet mine. "We will stop her. Together."

"Please be careful."

"I don't need to be. I have magic."

I forced a confident smile. "I know you do."

Killion picked up a final pawn and placed it on the map. "When the two are separated, the coven disabled, and the artifact destroyed, I will bring Chloe to the church and we will commence with Trinity's demise."

Katarina nodded. "I'll have my team there to make sure nothing and no one interferes." She grinned at me. "And then we'll have our party. You're passing out punch, Grave Girl."

I swallowed my dread. "If we pull this off tonight, I'll do whatever you want, Enforcer."

Katarina left, Andy headed to the kitchen to snag leftovers, and Aurora went into the bathroom to drink the potion and change into a suit similar to mine. "As you know, the robes will not accept anyone else," Killian said to me as we waited in the living room. "I had Harlow and Katarina find something close enough to pass."

We were on edge, our combined concerns tangling up my magic and words. My stumbling lexicon reminded me of when I'd finally began speaking again after my parents had passed. It had been a long, lonely road to return to the world of normal, and after months of mute grieving, my sentences often sounded like garbage. A knot sat in my heart, the threads of logic and love all balled up and getting tighter. Every time I tried to state what I was feeling, I failed. "Oh, Killion."

Even without me saying them, he knew what I wanted to express. He drew me into his arms and held me. "I know. Remember, not only are you and Aurora good at your jobs, but so am I. I've lived a long time. Seen a lot of conflicts, and if there's one thing I know, it's how my enemies think. My father made sure I would never underestimate them. No harm will come to me, nor the others tonight."

I stayed in the security of his embrace, trying to breathe and not cry. Just picturing about a young Killion being trained in the art of warfare made my heart hurt.

When Aurora emerged, Killion and I stared at her. My mouth dropped open.

With my eyes, she glanced down at herself, and then turned in a slow pivot. "Well? What do you think?"

"I can't believe it." It was as if I was looking at myself in a mirror. "That is wow on the up, and terrifying at the same time."

She arched a brow at the slang.

I shrugged. "Mason says it all the time."

"Solid," Andy said, exiting the kitchen with a half-eaten sandwich in hand. "If I didn't know it was you, I'd believe it was her."

"You'll need to fix your voice," Killion told her. "Lose the lilt."

"Right." She snapped her fingers and lowered her voice slightly, her speech becoming softer and less crisp. "I'm Chloe Frost, aka Grim Zero. Official badass and slayer of morons."

I screwed up my face. "Is that what I sound like?"

She had braided her hair, now brown and not as long as her normal strands, and twisted the end between her fingers, eyeing the purple lock. "None of us enjoy hearing our own voices."

I still couldn't wrap my mind around it. "I have to admit, this is impressive. Still terrifying, but impressive. I had no idea you could do this."

"You've seen me transform into a panther, but this is what awes you?"

"Yes."

She bowed at the waist. "I aim to please."

"What about the scythe?" Andy's cheek bulged as he chewed. "Trinity will be suspicious if Chloe Version Two is not carrying it."

"Version Two?" Aurora and I chorused at the same time.

He shrugged, swallowing. "What should I call you?"

"Aurora will do," she answered.

"We can't risk her getting her hands on the blade," Killion said. "While it may not harvest souls, as it would for the real Chloe"—his violet gaze slid to me and back and I felt his own incredulity at Aurora's likeness—"it is a dangerous weapon in its own right and contains a great deal of power. I did not have time to have an exact replica created, but I believe Death and I have something that comes close."

From the nearby armoire, he drew out a folded sickle. On the handle was a near identical skull and crossbones that matched my tattoo.

I fingered it, feeling the weapon's dull response. Death or Killion had infused it with magic, but it was a weak substitute for the true death blade.

I handed it to Aurora. "Keep it in the leather sheath if you can and no one will notice the difference." I tugged my shirt aside. "What about my tattoo? Again, it may not matter, but if she knows the grim mark and notices you don't have it, it could blow your cover."

She peeled her suit open to reveal a twin image. "My potions are top quality. I keep telling you this. Every mole, every freckle, and even your tattoo--they are all a match."

I chuckled. "I shouldn't doubt you, and I really don't, I just want to make sure we don't overlook anything. Your life is at stake, and I hate that you're going in place of me."

"I'll howl to that," Andy said.

"We should get going." Killion handed her the empty sheath. "The sun is setting."

If only I could stop time. I helped her strap the leather to her back and inserted the fake blade. I gave her a once over and declared her as close to my doppelgänger as she could get.

She and Andy walked out. "Catch you later," she called over her shoulder as I watched them enter the elevator. "Stay here and stay safe until we need you."

After the door closed, I turned in the doorway to Killion. He held my face with his hands and kissed me deeply. "Do not fret. All will be well. I give you my solemn promise."

"I can't tell you how much this sucks for me. I can't even be there as backup in case something goes wrong."

He stepped into the hall. "And because I know that's exactly what you will decide to do once I leave and you become even more anxious, I have invited a friend to sit with you."

"You did *what?*"

"Sorry, I'm late," Death said, materializing in the hall. "My squad is on standby. As soon as you give the word, they'll be there."

Killion nodded, heading for the elevator. My mouth hung open again, but before I could argue, my boss shoved me backward, waved Killion off, and closed the door. "Don't blame the bloodsucker," he yelled over my screech of indignation. "It was my idea."

"I hate you," I seethed.

He grinned and winked. "Don't kid yourself. You love me and you know it."

EIGHTEEN

You might think hanging out with Death would be entertaining, maybe even fun, listening to him tell you tales about his life and exploits.

You'd be wrong. It was boring as hell, and my anxiety was so high I wanted to use him as a punching bag. He'd warded all the doors and windows with his magic so I couldn't escape while he enjoyed a four-course meal prepared by Pennyworth. He insisted I sit across from him so he could keep an eye on me, and I amused myself with a butter knife, imagining all the ways I could use it on him.

He knew what I was thinking and would occasionally chuckle when I dug the end into the meal in front of me or caressed its blade with my thumb. "Relax," he told me. "The others will handle this. Believe it or not, they are quite capable without you."

With lightning speed, I threw the knife at his eye. He was too quick, catching it in midair before it struck its target. "Testy, too, I see. What is it with you and the Chloe Show? Not everything has to involve you."

"You need me to harvest Trinity." I gritted my teeth. "I *am* involved, you idiot."

"What happened to us trying harder to be friends? Do you really think I would send fang boy and the others into a situation they couldn't win?"

I gripped the edge of the table with my hands to keep from lunging at him. "I totally think that. While you pretend to like him, I know you'd be happy if he died."

He finished a piece of lobster roll, the end dripping with butter. "You're enough of a pain in my backside without me screwing you over in that manner." He gave me a disgruntled glance. "I don't need more hassle, and believe it or not, I've come to respect the vampire."

I sat back, itched to grab the knife again. "You're sure his plan will work?"

He wiped his lips with a napkin and covered the utensil with it. "Absolutely."

"Go check on them. See what's happening and report back. I need to know."

He narrowed an eye at me. "So you can attempt an escape? Come on. I may have pretended I didn't catch on to your manipulation regarding your employment agreement, but your acting skills aren't that good. You want me to leave so you can find a way out of here."

He had me on both counts. Reapers keepers, I thought I'd been so clever. All those months of making myself crazy, and he'd still figured it out. Or had he?

Time to tread carefully. I wanted to confirm he'd discovered my subterfuge, but did it matter? "You have the place warded. How could I possibly escape? And I may be a poor actor in your opinion, but I'm not stupid. I know how dangerous it would be for Trinity to get hold of me and my blood. I wouldn't take that chance and sentence everyone I love to death. That's what will happen, right? If she destroys the veil?"

"Not all will die. Some will be used for feedings, creating new hybrid species, torture."

"I can't believe SMG let this get so out of hand."

"You and me both."

He rarely said a word against Mei, the council, or the organization in general. I knew he had issues with them but he was a company man through and through.

Of course, he only had one job he was qualified for. No room for promotion or finding a different employer. Limited options made you resigned and careful. "Why didn't they step in sooner if they had any clue that this is what Trinity and Rag were attempting?"

He shrugged, emptying his third glass of wine. "Until you put it together, their alliance wasn't on SMG's radar. Even with that partnership in place, I don't think they dreamed such a collaboration could tear down the barrier between worlds. Normally, it couldn't. But with you in the mix?" He refilled the glass and shrugged. "The odds go up exponentially. Look, no matter what happens tonight, you'll be safe. I've made sure of it."

The tenor of his words caused me to taste iron and I swallowed hard. Unwelcome revelations took hold in my brain. "What did you do?"

"Your vampire is cunning on the battlefield, but he's never gone against a being like the mongrel. Angels are different. I needed to protect you in case the two of us are separated."

As I stared into his eyes, I felt woozy, as if I were the one who had downed a great deal of alcohol. My wine was untouched, his words echoing in my head even as the blood in my veins whooshed loudly in my ears. "Whatever you did..." I swallowed and blinked, suddenly forgetting my train of thought. *Killion. Aurora.* Were they in imminent danger? Dread threaded under my skin. "Check on them. Please. Send one of your team. Tinder, maybe."

"Tinder is on assignment elsewhere. Recruiting, in fact, for grim trainees." His voice began to sound far away, echo-y. "My squad needs to stay put. Even one person going off-script could endanger Killion's plan. All good generals know that."

Was he referring to himself? I swayed slightly, my jaw tingling. "Promise me Killion...will be...safe." My words came out mushy. "Matter...no...what."

"Chloe?" He frowned. "Are you okay?"

The room tilted. "Feel...sick."

Whap. My forehead hit the table and I was out.

The next thing I knew, I was standing in a graveyard, blinking at gray fog. A chilly breeze rustled the dying leaves on the trees and sent goosebumps over my exposed skin. My heartbeat echoed in my ears, my heart galloped with horrible anticipation.

Obsidian magic glittered under a blood moon. Trinity idled, leaning against a large concrete marker with two names engraved on it. At the pinnacle rested a bowed angel, a single tear ever-frozen on the concrete face. Still reeling, my stomach pitched when I recognized that angel. I'd picked it out, wishing I could turn to stone myself at that time. The gut-wrenching sensation hit my heart, crushing me with its weight. I knew exactly where I was. Who was buried at her feet.

My voice sounded odd, remote, but held icy command. "Get away from them."

She chuckled, sitting on the edge of the stone. Her cloak was missing and her gown had a plunging neckline that put her demon mark on display. It appeared still intact.

She crossed one leg over the other, her slinky red dress slit up the side. The fabric fell away from a long limb covered in black stockings. "There you are, Death Dealer, Queen of the Otherworld. I was worried you weren't joining the party."

My body quivered with rage and magic. No sight of her coven or Ragriel, but a pentagram glowed on the dried up lawn. I was smack in the center of it. "What game are you playing? How did you bring me here?"

"You doubt my power?" She stood and turned her attention to the ground, a red nail tracing the lines above the pentagram. It surged red and fiery. "The well of magic I now draw from amps up my abilities. In the early days, I could only move objects around. Now, I can move people. The wards on the hotel were challenging, but I still managed to bring your spirit here."

I felt the bodies of my mother and father tremble and wake—not because of her magic; no, they felt mine. It spun in ever tighter circles along with my mind, trying to work out how to kill her. More of the dead around us stirred. It wouldn't do to raise zombies when I was trapped inside the pentagram. I tried to calm myself, suffocate the necromancy.

Tried and failed. I wanted to raise the entire place and command them to descend on her. "But you're weak without your angel-demon boyfriend."

She hissed then waggled that red nail at me, contorting her lips from a grimace into a smile. "Riling me up won't work. I marked you that first time, you know, but it didn't take well. I had to up my game."

I glanced at my arm. The scratches were gone. If only I could get to her and do what Aurora had intended—deface hers. "I bare no mark by you, and you can't do anything to me with only my projection here."

"*Hir yw'r dydd a hir yw'r nos, a hir yw aros Arawn.* Long is the day and long is the night, and long is the waiting of Arawn. It's an old Welsh saying that I've repurposed, weaving my magic into it. It works like a locating spell for those I would use for my intents."

"Hey, sis!" Ragriel appeared, clapping his hands together as he offered a happy smile to Trinity. He wore no makeup tonight and appeared younger, less wrinkled. He looked me over. "She found you. This is good. Now we're all together."

My bones went cold. I mimicked Trinity's finger wag. "I know what you're doing, too, bringing me here. Making me feel vulnerable, emotional. We all know I'm not physically present. Neither are you two. You can't hurt me, nor use me for whatever you're planning, so what *is* this about, Ragriel?"

A brow arched. "I haven't heard that name in a long

time. You *are* a quick one, aren't you? See, here's the thing. I don't need your physical framework for this. Your astral body is perfectly satisfactory."

"For what?" I ground out.

The earth shook.

He grinned and before I could move, my arms and legs went immobile. A dissonant, chaotic energy flowed into me with the speed and precision of an injection. Through my spotted vision, I watched as he became nothing but mist and shadows.

I gagged as his razor-blade astral self slid down my throat, crammed into my nose, filled my ears. My body seemed to bloat as if someone had pumped me too full of air. My ribs cracked, my shoulders shook, my mind was shoved aside as he took over.

Everything within me screamed in outrage and then it all went distant, foggy. Unable to do more than breathe, my soul crouched in a dark corner, knowing it needed to hide. Hide from the darkness now sucking at my light. Hide from the maelstrom of raging hate and violence flooding my entire being.

Trinity made a sound of ecstasy.

Help...I called to Killion, Death.

It was weak. Too weak.

The hybrid was possessing me.

Ragriel laughed, feeling satisfied and...aroused?

Eww.

The echo of his laughter shot spiraling agony into my bones. I tried to lash out, shove him from my mind, but each time white-hot ice pierced into me. A migraine bloomed in my head.

After repeated attempts in rapid succession, I whimpered and cowed again. Black magic held me prisoner. "Time for us to take a little trip," he said as his too-cheery voice came through my lips. To Trinity, he added, "Prepare the circle."

With my eyes, which were now also his, I saw her smile, obsidian eyes flashing with glee. "I'll be waiting for your return. Tonight, we send you home."

In a heartbeat, he and I were in the penthouse, and I was sitting across from Death. Ragriel lifted my head from the table. It was as if no time had passed, and my boss eyed me with concern. "You don't look so good." He seemed to have no idea I'd called for help. "Can't hold your liquor, eh?"

Ragriel scanned the room, the detritus of the meal, the face across from him. A corona emanated from Death and awe washed over me at the sight of his wings. I'd only spotted them a few times before, but they always took my breath away.

Rag eased back, making a soft sighing sound. My body rippled and vibrated with his energy. "I've waited such a long while for this."

Death stilled at the odd intonation in my voice. "Chloe?"

With all my might, I shoved. I clawed. I screamed. Grim Zero sparked.

"*Help.*" It came out a whisper. Or maybe it was only in my mind. Rag smiled with my lips. "She's a bit...frozen at the moment."

"I see." Death toyed with the same knife I'd thrown at

him, no longer showing an ounce of worry. "Who then am I speaking to?"

Both evil and good flared inside me, battling with each other and roaring through me like a wildfire out of control. It was followed by crackling ice. My body twitched; Grim Zero flinched. *Fight*, she demanded.

Mentally panting, I lashed out with the small amount of magic I could gather. I sank claws into Ragriel's astral body, trying to hurt him the way he was me.

A howling filled my ears. I faltered, my weakened power slipping in and out of his haywire thoughts, but he slapped me away. Refusing to give in, I dug for every ounce of my being. I needed a foothold, anything that might help me exorcise him.

Exorcise. In the dregs of my mind, a faint thought tickled my brain. A passage in one of Aurora's books drifted out of the mental bedlam.

Why are you doing this? Grim Zero asked Ragriel. The spell that had drifted in slipped away. *This isn't the way home.*

He shuddered, her thought-words giving the angel inside pause. A tiny blue light, like a Fourth of July sparkler, flared to life.

And went out just as quickly. *Shut up, Death Dealer*, he replied. Then the demon in him surged, the hellfire in my veins alighting and raging again. *You won't trick us this time.*

Death Dealer. Only Trinity had called me that. Was she eavesdropping? Controlling the fire?

Grim Zero blanketed my insides with cool air. *I can give you peace.*

Across from me, Death continued to watch the war going on inside me. He tipped the knife end over end. "Hey, answer me. If you're not Chloe," he said, seemingly more curious than disquieted, "who are you?"

Ragriel twitched, causing one of my arms to randomly jerk, then a leg. A tick started under my left eye. He forced a tremulous smile, which felt like a grimace, and gripped the table to stop my hands from quivering. "You don't remember me? I'm hurt. Maybe this will jog your memory." He rose slowly from the seat and my shoulder blades felt like twin glass knives slit them from top to bottom. In my head, I screamed, as wings similar to Death's, sprouted and spread out to my sides. "Hello, brother."

NINETEEN

My teeth chattered; Ragriel clenched them.

Death continued playing with the knife. "Brother?" He snorted. "You're no relation of mine."

Faster than I could blink, Ragriel snatched it from Death's hand. He jammed it into the tabletop and growled. "It is my birthright as much as yours."

Pennyworth sashayed out of the kitchen, pulled up short at seeing me in such a state. Sensing a threat, but confused since it looked like me, he produced a wicked-looking meat cleaver and flashed it around. "Need assistance, Master Death?"

My boss shook his head. "I've got it. Leave us, and tell your friend his package is safe."

Something flickered in the butler's eyes. A message, but I couldn't decipher it with the battle of wills going on inside me. He disappeared out of the room and I heard the front door close sharply.

Ragriel bared his teeth—*my* teeth. "I'm going home and you're going to help me."

"Sorry, mate. I don't work with half-breeds."

At the distasteful term, the rage inside Ragriel exploded like a nuclear bomb. I whimpered. "You owe me," he snarled, slamming my hands down. A seismic wave rolled through the room and the heavy, solid table cracked down the middle. "You help me or your favorite plaything dies."

Now *I* was the one to bristle, although it was a fleeting emotion as I was again buffeted by his whiplash energy. Like riding river rapids, I was tossed, battered into rocks, drowned, only to be thrown into the air and land again in the subjugating waters of his conflicting magics.

Death casually slid the chair back and crossed an ankle over one knee. "We've been here before, the three of us. You know how this will end."

He was my only lifeline and I reached for him, distantly wondering why he wasn't more upset. Why he wasn't attacking Ragriel and trying to save me.

My possessor held out both hands. "This time is different. I have the advantage."

A soft glow in the palm of one caught my attention, although neither of them seemed to notice it. As I stared at the tiny flickering light, I remembered how it felt when Death cut the skin there and our blood and magics had mingled only hours ago.

We'd been in these same spots. Squaring off. Him agreeing to my proposal in a manner that now seemed too easy. I'd thought I had manipulated him, but somehow he'd done it to me.

His earlier words skittered across my brain. *I needed to protect you in case the two of us are separated.* Had he meant by physical location, or in this manner—unable to communicate?

I trudged through the chaos, searching for Grim Zero's brightness. She had gathered her power, coiled it inward. *What did he do?* I asked her as Death said, "Killing her will also kill any possible bridge home."

Rag muttered curses, flapped his wings.

Grim Zero said, *Can't you feel it?*

In the midst of this possession? I grappled at her suggestion. I felt far too much and yet my own self seemed dim, my magic fading faster and faster under the assault.

As Ragriel argued with Death, I fell down, down, down. Into the depths of the original grim. I'd been here before and never imagined it would be a refuge, yet I was drowning in it and relieved to be so. For a brief moment, clarity struck. My attention fixated on Death's glowing corona, his wings. Each feather glistened, whispered to me. As I felt their divineness, I was lifted up through the watery, emotional depths of Grim Zero, and anchored against the raging power of Ragriel.

In my mind's eye, I felt the power. Not grim power. Not vampire.

Death's.

It spread in my veins with lethal speed, eating up Rag's as if it was a Pac-Man gobbling power pellets. Just like those pellets, it grew in energy, becoming a thing all on its own, filling me with white light. The spell came to me, fully formed.

The demon-angel stiffened and cursed loud enough to shake the overhead chandelier with his scream. "No!"

A new fight ensued, but the light mixed with Grim Zero's power and I became unstoppable. My wings—not his—spread like the beautiful, commanding life force they were. My body jackknifed, head falling back as I laughed. With my new, improved vision, I could see through the roof into the night sky. If I'd wanted to, I could have flapped my wings, and flown past the moon, the stars.

"I bring you forth from the dark and hold you to the light." The words spilled from my lips, my own voice reinstated. "I meet and greet you with open arms, my brother, and I move you back into the light."

He cried out again, a mixture of horror from his demon and relief from his angel. Ghosts rose around me, the dead long buried under layers and layers of ground beneath us coming to life. "I move you all into the light," I said. Dozens of blue sparks danced in my peripheral vision. "You are all mine. The time has come for you to go home."

The building trembled. The spirits wailed. Ragriel surged out of me, his demon unable to stay and his angel hovering above the table, staring down at me. "If only this would work," he said.

And then he vanished.

The trembling stopped. The ghosts faded away. The wings disappeared.

Death, still seemingly unconcerned, honed in on me. "Chloe?"

"What just happened?" I blinked. "Where did he go?"

"Where he belongs." His gaze swept over me. "Trippy being an angel, isn't it? I wasn't sure you were going to come back from the edge."

My mouth tasted like metal and feathers. The odd scent of infinity clung to my nose. "Neither was I. Gotta say, I'm having serious misgivings about another year of this stuff." Like a melting icicle, I sank into the seat. "Is it over?"

Death's aura was no longer visible to me. Nor were his wings. "Too soon to tell."

"Why didn't you help me?"

He sat back, perplexed. "I injected you with some of my essence. You'd be nothing but a puddle of brain goo if I hadn't."

"You should've done more." Although, I wasn't sure exactly what that would've been. How do you top getting a shot of angel mojo? "Did you anticipate he would possess me?"

"That's what he does—body jumps. Didn't you read the file? He technically doesn't have a physical flesh and blood form, so he has to take someone else's. It seemed prudent to make sure he couldn't jump in and control you, and I thought my angel essence would be enough to keep him out. It would have if he'd tried to simply hop into your meat suit. He's never piggybacked onto a projection before. That's new. Probably Trinity's idea."

From the fragments I'd seen in his mind, I knew he

was smart, yet constantly too agitated to focus. Trinity was both highly intelligent and devious.

Flesh and blood. My brain hung on the words, but I didn't know why. "Why didn't you warn me?"

"When I infused you, I didn't know what was about to go down, nor had Killion and I discussed his strategy. It was simply a precaution. One I hoped you'd never need."

My outrage dulled. A part of me thought I should thank him. "We've exchanged blood before. Why didn't I get some of your angel DNA then?"

"It's not tangible like that. More like...part of my soul. It's not of this world."

I rubbed the hollow spot between my breasts. "Why were you so cruel to him?"

Once again, he gave me a perplexed look. "After everything he's done, you're worried about his feelings?"

I'd felt how hurt he'd been at Death's rejection. At the cutting expression Death had used. "Maybe one of the reasons he's gone to the dark side is because everyone has been hateful to him. Having been inside his head, I can tell you, he's a wacko, but he wasn't lying—he's searching for home. Whatever that is. He needs someone to show him the way."

"You sent him to the light. Best we can do."

Was it? "The light as in heaven?"

A shrug. "The Christian version of the afterlife? Sure. That works."

"SMG doesn't have him imprisoned somewhere?"

"He's not here, that's all I care about. We harvest this witch and we're golden."

"I don't feel golden. He needs help, not a jail cell."

Death placed an elbow on the table and pointed a finger at me. "You'd be wise to keep your nose out of it."

A flash of anger caught in my belly. "Is that a threat?"

"A warning. There are things going on—things I can't discuss—but that I'm looking into. If you go sniffing around, the evidence I need might disappear."

The anger fled. Confusion took root. My migraine pounded. "Evidence for what?"

He seemed pained, running a hand over his face. "Let's say that his creation was no accident."

"I don't know what that means."

He gave me a flat look.

I gave it right back to him. We rarely shared the open telepathy he and Grim Zero had experienced as soul-mates, and that Killion and I now enjoyed. There were moments, however, when the inner workings of his mind were clear enough. "You think someone contrived for an angel and a demon to hook up and produce offspring?"

His mouth firmed, and then, deciding he'd said too much, he let out an exasperated sigh. "There is no Mama and Papa in this scenario. He's the original test tube baby. Probably one of a dozen or more, but he's the only viable result."

My tired brain twisted and spun, trying to reason out his meaning. "Someone is experimenting with angel and demon essence? Mixing them together."

He touched the end of his nose in a *bingo* gesture. "Nephilim are a breed apart, but Ragriel? He's a one of a kind mistake, and hopefully not reproducible."

"But you're worried he's not a one-off." Maybe that's why I felt a bond to him. I still wanted to rage at him for what he'd done, but there was a thin, tenuous bond, because like me, he was an anomaly. "Who would do that and why?"

"The who is what I'm investigating. The why? To create a volatile weapon. That's all I can come up with. My first order of business is trying to figure out who's behind it; secondly, I need to make sure they aren't performing more experiments. One Ragriel in this world is more than enough. Can you imagine if they created an army?"

"Surely, they can see their result had serious flaws. If anything, he's a failure."

"In our minds, yes. He's obviously hard to control, but if Trinity *does* have a way of doing it, she may be the next who's experimented on."

My stomach clenched. I wished I could close my eyes, forget about this. Wished it was a horrible night-mare that would end when I woke up.

Chloe? It was Killion.

Sensing the master vampire was calling, Death left me and strolled into the kitchen.

Me: *I'm here.*

Killion: *What happened? I couldn't reach you, but Pennyworth claimed you were safe.*

The "package" Death had mentioned to the butler. I rubbed my chest, feeling disheartened and also double-crossed. *I was possessed by Ragriel, but I kicked him out, and I sprouted wings. He's gone. So are they.*

I was a touch sad about that last fact.

The Romanians love their curses and have elevated swearing to an art form. Sarcasm, as well. I was pretty sure his next diatribe over my confession had to do with sending the hybrid to the devil and making him eat something foul. *You're all right?*

From the other room came the sounds of cabinets opening and closing. Death returned with a bottle of Killion's favorite whiskey and a squat glass.

Me: *I will be. You?*

Killion: *So far, so good. Where's the demon? I will torture and kill him. Slowly.*

Me: *Not sure.*

Killion <silence>: *He's on the loose?*

Me: *I sent him to the light, trying to save him. He disappeared, so fingers crossed.*

Killion: *You tried to save* him?

My boss poured a shot and handed it to me. My stomach revolted. *I'll explain later. What's happening there?*

Killion: *We've trapped the witch. Her coven has not surfaced, however. Aurora has sliced through the mark and is working on disconnecting the spirit bag from Yonah. So far, no success.*

More sadness gripped me. *I'll meet you at St. Anne's as soon as I can stand and we'll send Trinity on her way.*

Killion: *See you soon. I want to hear about the wings.*

I downed the liquor, grimacing. Then I rose on unsteady legs, staggered, sat again. "Killion has Trinity. We need to get to the church."

"You need to recover first," Death poured another finger of whiskey. "It's not every day you get to experience the magnificence of me."

I didn't have the energy to roll my eyes. "Why is it gone? Your angelic power?"

"Sharing is forbidden. That was a small sip, you might say, and you used it up expelling Ragriel. You must never tell anyone, do you understand? This is between us."

Oops. I'd have to make sure Killion never spilled the beans about me sprouting wings. I gave a nod and downed the second shot. It burned my throat, but the heat it spread was comforting, nothing like Ragriel's—Trinity's—blistering fire. "I feel sorry for him. If what I experienced is what he's been going through every day since he was created..." I shuddered. "How has he not exploded from the pressure?"

"Trinity, remember?"

I considered what I'd witnessed during the possession. A new thought hit. The exhaustion wouldn't let it sink in, though. It floated away like a feather on the breeze. "Doesn't seem she's doing him any favors."

Death shrugged. "Can you imagine how bad he would be without her?"

Once again, I considered the fact that everything we'd initially assumed about the two of them had been wrong. The previous errant thought nudged my brain again. "What if her magic *isn't* controlling his chaos? What if she's convinced him it is, but in reality, she's making it worse?"

"For what purpose?"

"I don't know." I was simply too tired to make sense of it. "I need my robes and scythe."

"I'll get them."

"No." I waved him off. "I've got it."

My legs were rubbery but my magic stirred at the sight of my tools. It took me far longer than normal to pull on the suit and I had to rest on the edge of the bed more than once and breathe. My palm heated, lusting after the handle of the death blade, and the migraine throbbed. Anxiety continued to thrum in my veins and I knew none of us could relax until I had harvested the witch. "This isn't over," I told Death when I rejoined him. I swayed on my feet. "I can feel it."

Placing an arm around my waist, he snatched up the whiskey bottle and walked me to the door. "We better get to the church then," he said. "Fast."

TWENTY

Death decided I was too fragile for a trip through space. Luckily, even though it was nearing midnight, we found a familiar ride service driver waiting for us.

"Rafael?" I staggered, as he emerged from the driver's seat. "What are you doing here?"

His car idled in the hotel's circular drive and he'd decorated it with skeleton legs dangling from the trunk and a plastic pumpkin hanging from the rearview. Dressed as a vampire, he offered a small wave over the hood. His fake teeth made him lisp. "Your boyfriend texted and said you needed a lift. I got here as fast as I could." In this rare instance, he could see Death, who normally stayed invisible around mundanes. Rafael's dark brows dipped at the possessive hold my boss had around me, and the half-empty bottle in his hand. "Are you drunk?"

I laughed, the sound harsh. "Nope. I've come down with a virus." Lying had become far too easy in the past year. I waited for the twinge of guilt, but it didn't surface. "I'm a touch woozy from it. Did my boyfriend give you the address?"

Rafael rushed to open the rear door for us. "And a nice fat tip. You tell him I am available to drive you and him around town *anytime*."

The early model Corolla had seen better days. Even when it had been brand new, it would have been no competition for the limo. "He's a generous guy. I'll be sure to let him know."

Cat hair coated the seat and collected on my pants as he drove us to the church. Quite a change from the first time I'd met him and he'd refused to allow animals in his vehicle. The funny thing was, his cat, Veronica, peered at us from the front, her sharp eyes lingering on Death. I'd accidentally resurrected her before I had control of my necromancy and my boss had given her a subsequent "grooming" since she'd been slightly flat and smelled like carrion. He'd made her look less like roadkill and more like a pretty kitty, totally enchanting Rafael.

The younger trick-or-treaters were already home and probably in sugar comas by now. A few teens still combed the sidewalks. Rafael made small talk while I mentally replayed the meeting between me and Trinity at my parents' burial site. Along with that, random other memories dropped in and faded out. I kept losing the thread of conversation, thanks to my raging headache and ping-ponging thoughts, but was relieved when Death covered for me and kept Rafael engaged.

All was dark when we arrived, and the heavy dread, along with my pulse, kicked up a notch. Rafael leaned forward to peer out the windshield. A murky haze draped itself over the top spires. What little moonlight forcing its way through only illuminated the broken and decaying sidewalk. The statue of Our Virgin Mary at the steps to the entrance listed sideways. Someone had placed a black pointed hat on her head, and she seemed to mock both Halloween and The Catholic Church. Rafael removed his fake teeth. "You sure this is where you want me to let you out?"

The bar across the street was packed with drunken revelers in costumes, spilling onto the sidewalk. Voices and laughter floated to us and I spotted three familiar faces.

"Ghouls," I muttered.

Rafael followed my gaze, but luckily thought I'd said something else. "Yeah, girls. Lots of them. In costumes." He sighed wistfully.

Death opened the door, focused on the church, and said, "You should go talk to the one in the cowgirl getup."

Rafael stuttered, embarrassed, as I accepted Death's hand and scooted across the seat. The driver combed fingers through his hair in a nervous gesture. "I mean, I'm not really into the bar scene."

"Me neither." I leaned through the open passenger window. "The Smoking Bean is doing a special coffee tasting tomorrow. You might find somebody interesting there."

He scratched the cat's head, nodding. She purred softly but kept her gaze leveled on my boss behind me. "I could stay, if you need a ride home."

Death drew me away. "Not tonight, Romeo. Hit the

bar or the coffee shop. Go home. Whatever. Don't hang out here."

I gave him a *sorry* face and watched them drive off, Veronica craning her neck out the window to peer at us. "You didn't need to be rude," I chastised Death. "He's lonely."

"You can't fix everyone, Chloe."

He ogled the church again. As usual, I could see its magical glow caused by the glamour Killion kept on it. To the causal mundane observer, it appeared to be a deserted brick monstrosity with a private cemetery that dominated most of a block. To those of us with magic, it loomed like a phantom in the night, sometimes more solid than others, but projected power and superiority, much like the master vampire who owned it.

Death's eyes narrowed. "Quiet, isn't it?"

I lowered my voice, the cool night air chilling my face—an unwelcome reminder of Ragriel's frozen tundra and cracking pools of ice. "Maybe they're lying in wait for the coven. Killion and the vamps probably made themselves invisible. Let's get inside."

I reached out with my telepathy. *Killion? We're here.*

Before we could get up the steps, Trinity appeared in front of us. "I've been waiting for you, and you brought a friend." She offered Death a coquettish face. "I feared my channel had failed."

Killion? Why is the witch out here?

The master vampire didn't answer and my guts crawled. "Ragriel? He didn't," I told her, shoring up my strength. What had she done to Killion and the others? I could barely stop myself from rushing up the stone steps and flinging myself into the church to find out.

Chloe, Killion said in my mind. *The witch is trapped inside the nave.*

Relief at his voice swamped me. "Ah, I see," I said to her, knowing he was listening and would hear me. "You're playing games again. You really have a jones for astral projection, don't you?"

"Do you live in a cave?" Her hard gaze flicked to me, back to Death. "No one uses that word anymore."

"Are you schooling me?"

"What was it like being possessed?" She licked her lips as if she could taste my emotions. "Frightening? Terrifying?"

I locked my knees so my legs didn't wobble. Being possessed had left me nearly powerless; I wouldn't allow the memory to do the same. "Funny enough, I caught fragments of insight into him *and* you. I'm in awe of your ability to outwit us. Your trickery and guile are truly inspiring."

This surprised her, making her smile falter.

I went on. "He's your twin, isn't he? He saved you that night you accidentally caused the fire that killed your parents and destroyed his flesh and bones container." Images from his memory snapped into place, as if Grim Zero were putting the pieces of the puzzle together in my head. "He body jumped into a passing stranger, forcing him to rescue you. The man had no recollection of it afterward, but you lived and Ragriel continued to possess others as you grew so he could stay close to you. A symbiotic relationship, you fed each other magically."

The smile fell completely off her face. She opened her mouth, but clamped it shut as I went on. Death zeroed in on me, listening closely.

"That blemish." I pointed to her exposed skin. I could see where Aurora had left a thin line through it. "It's no demon's mark; it's from a burn that you received in the fire. You wanted others to fear you, so you made up that story, and you also lied to Rag, telling him you'd help control his powers and find a way to get him *home*, when in reality, you've used him for your own purposes to gain power and bring hell to earth through destruction and mayhem."

A fresh smile teased her lips. She was proud of herself.

"Home is a feeling, not a place, so each instance you told Rag to possess someone new and *this time* it would work and he would feel whole, he believed you because he longed for it so deeply. With his original vessel gone, though, and since your souls were contrived in a cosmic Petri dish rather than having been created from love, there was never a way for him to feel at home, was there?"

My blood tingled almost painfully with the energy of vampires en masse joining us. As suspected, they were keeping themselves invisible. Killion was close, sending me a wave of his magic. He, too, was listening intently.

Trinity twisted her fingers through the air. Remnants of Ragriel's frenzied energy crystallized inside me, turning to a flame and sucking the air in my lungs. I'd forgotten the crystal Aurora had given me, but reached for my own magic. Due to Ragriel, it wasn't normal, and the pain behind my eyes grew as I snagged the sharp, broken pieces, attempting to mend them. The flame grew but Grim Zero sent a soothing coolness to smother it. Free again, I inhaled a lung full of fresh oxygen. Trinity frowned as I smiled through the throbbing in my head and the aches in my body. "Nice try, but ask anyone—I'm hard to kill."

The debate in her gaze was plain. She knew she'd been had, but refused to give up. She had more tricks.

I tapped the death blade in the palm of my hand, narrowing my eyes and pushing against her protected layers of magic. "You kept Rag in a state of madness, taking off the edge enough when you needed him to do something for you. And all the while you convinced him you cared for him."

Killion's energy cocooned me. The last of her evil magic receded.

"You're the ultimate score," she said, her voice warm syrup over sandpaper, regardless of her uncertainty. She wasn't talking to me, however. Her stare pinned my boss.

I glanced at Death, as cool and confident as ever. Bored, even. "That's what I keep telling people, but they don't believe me." A corner of his mouth twitched. "Can we get on with this? There's a gal in a cowboy costume over there who's in need of a real man tonight." He winked.

I gaped. "Seriously? That's what's on your mind at the moment?"

"I'm afraid you're going to have more important things to attend to." Trinity's voice turned flirty again.

"But if you want a few hours of fun, I'll be available later."

OMG. They almost deserved each other. "Look, Trin, you don't have your artifact and your master is gone," I told her. "Your plan for bringing down the veil is over. I told you that you wouldn't win this fight." I flashed the scythe. "Now take it like a good witch and let's get this over with."

She laughed, knives of fury scratching at my skin. "My master isn't Ragriel, you stupid girl, and like I told you, he'll never allow you to harvest me."

A finger of dread resurfaced in my gut. Aurora's words echoed in my mind. *She doesn't seem the type to mess with higher order beings, only lower ones.* "Ragriel got more angel mojo and you got more demon in those Petri dishes, but you convinced him he was the evil one, didn't you?"

"What does it matter now? I'm free." She dropped her attention to my chest. "You, with your ridiculous emotions, aren't. I needed to test my spell to capture you, so the first time I used a random family to draw you to me. Then I discovered your parents were dead. Much stronger magic and your emotions opened you up to my brother like a child does their mouth for candy."

It was good intel for the coming year of service to SMG, but the fact she'd brought my parents into this filled me with rage. I would not, however, let her goad me into foolishness. "You caught me there." From the corner of my eye, I saw movement. The ghoul queen slithered out of the shadows. Her minions across the street broke from the bar crowd and moved in our direction, as well. "But I'm afraid, Trinity, our time is up. At least, yours is."

More ghouls appeared. Hunger lit their eyes, lips curling around rows of sharp teeth. For a heartbeat, I froze, unsure who their target was. Us or Trinity?

Bong. While the church's bell had been silent for decades, it rang now, the resonant sound loud and ominous. Trinity puffed out of sight, then reappeared ten feet away. She laughed back at me. Beyond, the cemetery beckoned and I felt things long dead stir. "*Your* time may be up," she called. "Mine is just beginning."

Another peal of the bell. I glanced at Death, knowing midnight was upon us. His face was taut. "What is your goal, here?" he yelled after her. "To bring down the veil? You won't survive."

She blinked out again, reappeared, the magical residue becoming the fog she so loved to use. Her projection went right through the invisible vampires. "Not only will I survive, I'll rule over all the dark things. It's too late to stop it." She flicked one of those red nails at the cemetery gate. "The veil is already ripping to shreds."

Menacing clouds appeared overhead. I rushed to keep her in sight as the magical fog thickened, wrapping itself around me and the others. It separated us, the stench of dead things, sulfur, and smoke making me gag. I heard the ghouls gnashing their teeth; following. They trailed after her, though, not me, and I realized too late, as they disappeared into the murky haze, that they wanted flesh.

The bodies in the cemetery had long been buried and probably held little appeal. So what *were* they after?

What did she mean that the veil had already been ripped?

"Chloe! Come back," Death yelled.

At the same time, Killion was in my head. *Do not follow her!*

My instincts clanged as loudly as the bell, telling me to run the other direction, but even if I'd wanted to backtrack, I couldn't because of the thick fog. I knocked into a grave marker and went down on one knee, pain gripping my leg. I cursed, limping back to my feet. Most of my energy had returned, but the thick shadows closed in and a wave of suffocating claustrophobia came over me. I turned in circles, trying to get my bearing.

Killion, I can't find my way out.

Him: *Stay where you are. I'm searching for your magic. She's using an illusion to confuse all of us. Can you see anything that might help me locate you?*

I bent down close enough to read the grave marker. *Edwin Bertram. I'm at his burial plot, probably two sections deep into the yard.*

A shiver of wind blew past and a slender piece of sky cleared. The moon spotlighted Trinity on top of a mausoleum, hands raised upward and lips moving as she uttered a spell. The ghouls gathered below, near frantic, like fan girls at a concert. They reached for her, for the sky.

I heard a tearing noise, a renting of the air. My ears popped, my stomach recoiled. She was pulling down the veil. I couldn't stay at the marker—I had to stop her.

As I ran all out toward the throng, I saw her coven emerge from the hedgerows. The rip grew into an enormous laceration above and I skidded to a stop, my blood freezing at the sight of what peered down at her, at the others.

At me.

She turned and met my eyes, hers blazing red. "Meet my master, Death Dealer. He's been waiting for you."

TWENTY-ONE

The thing that climbed out from the other side of the veil was massive, thick-muscled, all claws and shark teeth. It sported curling horns, one on each side of its block-sized head.

With scales for skin and a whipping tail, it towered over us, resembling a movie monster ready to destroy a city. My neck cricked from trying to look at it.

"Get to the church." Killion, who'd caught up to me, jerked me away from the approaching demon. "Harvest Trinity."

I stumbled and fell, my brain and body in shock as more demons poured through the opening. Some crawled, others flew. Killion brandished a sword as the cemetery filled with his vampires, shifters, and more ghouls. In one swift movement, he lifted me to my feet, placed a kiss on my forehead, and propelled me toward the exit.

I wanted to grab him and force him to come with me, my new fear so fierce, I could barely think straight. All I wanted to do was protect him, but if I did that, everyone else would perish.

Death stood at the gate, eyes closed, and lifted his arms. His lips were moving and a bubble rose around the area to contain the beasts. They screeched when they struck it, some attempting to scale it, but finding no escape.

"Don't you dare let Killion die," I screamed at him as I sprinted for the church steps.

I took them two at a time, my speed slowed only by my glance at the battle going on behind me. The clash of good and evil was deafening, and I nearly stumbled again when I saw one of the demons grab Mason and throw him into the air. "No!" I shrieked, but he fell and disappeared among the others, and it took all my willpower not to race back to the fighting.

Swallowing sick desperation, I hit the thick wooden doors, flinging them aside. They banged against the walls and Ghost met me, panting in her psychopomp form. Drool dripped from her mouth and she barked, nipping at my heels as I raced to the nave.

Katarina and Harlow guarded the witch, who was seated and chained. Trinity's face was bemused, her eyes unfocused, her body slack.

"It's not ready yet," Aurora cried from the bench where she worked, still appearing as my twin, as I lunged with the scythe. "Yonah is still—"

"No time," I told her. "She dies now."

"What's happening out there?" Harlow asked.

I couldn't meet her eyes. "There's a tear in the veil. It doesn't look good."

Katarina's fangs showed as she snarled. "The master?"

I raised the weapon. "He could use your help."

She snatched up a machete. Harlow unslung the crossbow from her back. Neither had taken two steps, nor had I managed to swing the death blade, when the side of the church was struck by a massive blow.

Bricks, mortar, and stained glass exploded and rained down, the impact lifting us off our feet and tossing us through the air. The sizable hole allowed the scaly demon to step inside, debris crunching under his massive foot. The thing peered down at us and Trinity cheered.

The ongoing war outside grew louder, dust clogging my throat, the stench of the otherworldly creature invading my nose. Killion and Andy sprinted in behind the monster, hopping over debris. Killion's gaze searched for me and we locked eyes.

End this, he commanded.

Coughing and forcing myself to stand while ignoring the pain and torment inside, I raised the scythe once more.

Katarina had taught me well—no matter how big, gruesome, or fast your opponent, find a way to use their strengths against them. *Knees, hands, eyes.* Those were the strategic points the enforcer had drilled into me when facing an enemy. "You two"—I pointed at her and Harlow, both in full vampire mode as they regained their feet. Their eyes were wide with shock at the sight of the beast—"cut him off at the knees."

If your opponent couldn't walk, he couldn't reach you.

Instantly, each went into a strategic posture, wielding their weapons. The monster's knees were as tall as Death, and it would be no easy feat to cut the tendons to strike it down.

I scanned quickly for my doppelgänger but Aurora was lying in a heap of rubble. Her eyes stared vacantly at the ceiling. I suffocated my cry and turned to the master vampire. If your opponent couldn't use his hands to hold a weapon or grab you, he had less chance of inflicting serious injury. "Killion, you and Andy sever the hands."

It was too bad the Undead couldn't fly like so many legends claimed. Killion could still leap higher than anything in nature. Andy morphed into his wolf. Killion grabbed him by the scruff, and the two became invisible. Ghost howled.

The beast, who'd focused on them, howled back its displeasure. The reverberation shook the weakened walls and more crumbled. Dust and magic coated everything. Before the noise ended, the others attacked.

It took Katarina three swipes to cut through the scaly skin at the back of the monster's left knee. Harlow sunk bolts into the right in rapid fashion.

As one leg gave out and the creature crashed down on its useless patella, its left hand was sliced clean off. It wailed, trying to shake off its unseen attacker, yet the eyes zeroed in on me. As Andy became visible, leaping onto the other arm, green goo ran from the severed limb. The right wrist was flayed open by vicious fangs.

I charged for the witch. *Kill*, my scythe sang.

Yes, I answered, but smacked into a wall of obsidian magic.

Trinity's eyes were all black when she turned them on me. Although she seemed unconcerned about her master and its injuries, she cursed me in that ancient language she loved, the words rolling off her tongue with practiced ease.

I whacked at her magic, cleaving it enough to gain a foothold inside the pentagram. I wanted to stop the destruction she had initiated, but I wanted to make her suffer for what she'd done just as much. "Call them off," I ordered, reaching right through her protective shield and grabbing her by her dress. I hoisted her from the chair, the chains bringing it with her body as I squared off with her nose to nose. "You've lost."

While I'd interrupted her spell, her lips curled in a smile. "Have I?"

The floor shook. The beast, though nearly incapacitated, lunged at me. It managed to grab me and lift me from the ground, my feet flailing as I screamed.

"Hey, big guy," a familiar voice said.

My voice.

I glanced over my shoulder and saw Aurora staggering to standing. The imitation suit was ripped, her face dirty and bruised. Blood leaked from her nose. "I'm the real grim reaper."

Trinity wasn't confused but the beast was. It dangled me, its attention sliding to her, back to me.

Those horns were far too close to my face, but those eyes—they weren't soulless like Trinity's. They were familiar and I sucked in a breath as realization struck. "Yonah?"

It came out a shocked whisper, but the beast heard.

While the massive hand closed around my torso, crushing the air from my lungs, the others renewed their attacks on it.

The tumult going on around me disappeared. My astral self landed on my back at the elder's burial site, the yellow tape flapping in the breeze. I scrambled to my feet. Offerings were piled around the grave, candle flames flickering.

"Help me," her spirit said, floating a few feet away. "The horrors I have seen in that demon..."

The demon had her inside it. Not possession like I'd experienced, but close enough. I bit back my rage and sorrow, along with the frustration at my consciousness being here rather than the church. I couldn't save her, but I needed to save my friends. "I'm sorry, I don't know how. We've done everything we can but if I don't harvest that witch, everyone will die. I have to go back."

"My granddaughter. Tell her to sing my favorite song."

Um...okay. "Is there something about it that will help you?"

"No." Her smile was sad but filled with surrender to her fate. "But it will remind me I was human, as well as coyote."

I felt a constriction around my chest. I couldn't breathe. The next heartbeat I was back in my body, being crushed by the demon.

Kill, the sword sang.

My tattoo heated.

I had to kill the beast.

And sacrifice Yonah to do it.

Death! Save the elder for me. Whatever price I have to pay, I'll do it.

As the beast fought Killion, Death popped in with Pepper and Farina. "You called?"

Me: *How did you know?*

Death: *My skills are so underrated.*

Me: *Tell her to sing her grandmother's favorite song.*

He shrugged and relayed the info. Pepper, too pale and bloody gave me a blank look and then at my choking nod, relented. "*Somewhere...over the rainbow,*" her voice rang out sure and true. Farina joined in.

The beast checked itself. We were still face to face, its attention boring into me. *I'm sorry I couldn't do more,* I told Yonah and hoped she understood.

Its visage drew close, breath reeking of sulfur and heating my skin. "Corvus," I yelled, fighting the restriction in my lungs. My ribs felt crushed. The bird swooped in from outside, winging its way into the high open ceiling before dive-bombing us. "Kill," I muttered.

I pointed at one of the eyes, and by the time he aimed his beak for it, I drew back my blade and went for the other.

We struck in unison. Soundless, the beast froze, then fell forward in slow motion. As it did, I reached in with my necromancy, pushing past Trinity's possession of it, searching for Yonah's spirit.

The evil essence inside was all Trinity. It shook and gnashed at me, clawing at my mind, but the entity itself was nothing but a shell that she had possessed and used against us. Like her own physical vessel that had been born in a magical test tube, it lacked a soul of its own.

I caught the faintest flicker of a spirit, a blue spark, tiny wings fast as a hummingbird beating frantically. *Yonah.* Sending out a pulse of my magic, I filled the creature with it, shoving back Trinity's obsidian shards and reaching for the spark. *Come to me.*

By the time the beast finished crashing facedown, squashing me like a bug, I had her.

I don't know the way, she said, her ghostly face frowning with confusion.

I do, I told her. *Follow me.*

Yep, I was a spirit now, too, and since I couldn't take her hand and lead her out of the monstrous container, I simply went up.

We floated above the others and watched as Trinity was surrounded by vampires and shifters, but they were all fighting her monsters. Killion raged against a demon who moved through space like shadows with no corporeal form. The master vampire sliced and whirled to keep up with it, then he simply vanished, turning himself invisible. The demon, perplexed, stopped and glanced around. A heartbeat later, it lost its head.

Ghost was the only one who noticed me, her giant muzzle lifting to track me and my charge. Trinity saw it and slid her black eyes in our direction. Aurora lunged for the witch and Trinity hit her with a spell that sent her flying through the air.

No, I yelled through ghostly lips, but no one heard except Yonah. My friend's body crumpled onto a pile of bricks. Pepper and her sister shoved at the fallen beast, trying to roll him off me. Katarina, bloodied and limping, assisted them. I couldn't find Harlow, Andy, or Mason.

Such horror, Yonah said, *that spark of her soul still quivering like tiny wings. I'm sorry.*

Not your fault. I nodded for Ghost to prepare. *It's time for you to be at peace.*

The psychopomp reared back, preparing to leap. *Are you coming with me?* Yonah asked.

I have to stay. I caught sight of Death from the corner of my eye. He was throwing demons out of the way like they were tennis balls as he stomped toward Pepper and the others. *Your friends and family will be on the other side.*

Ghost leaped.

Yonah: *Tell Pepper and Farina I love them.*

Me: *I will.*

As the psychopomp went insubstantial to escort Yonah's soul to the afterlife, Trinity used her magic to reach for mine.

I had no physical form, no scythe, and no psychopomp. There were no rules or strategies for handling this.

Her spell broke over me, tugging at my spirit. She grinned maniacally, turning her hands over and over, reeling me in.

I didn't fight it. Death used his magic to flip the beast off me, dropping to his knees next to my mangled corpse. Any second I was going to pop back into it and give Trinity a surprise.

Except, I didn't. My ghost hovered in front of her. She opened her mouth wide and swallowed me whole.

TWENTY-TWO

The chaos I had experienced inside Ragriel was nothing compared to what made its home inside of her.

Fire consumed me with wave after wave of hate and rage. I floundered, my spirit trying to hold onto something good. To not be swallowed up by her flames, her desire to destroy everything.

I reached for Killion. For Death. For Aurora.

Somewhere over the rainbow...

I latched on to the shaky voices of the sisters, tearful, but still filled with hope.

Others joined them. More and more. A whole chorus.

The flames singed me, ate away at my brain, ripped through my heart trying to incinerate it. Grim Zero was there, fighting with me, taking up the song and amplifying it in my brain.

There's a land that I heard of...

My own soul flickered, sputtered, died. The flames leapt with delight.

Fight her. Killion's voice was a command in my head. In my heart. *Turn her strength against her*.

Anger. Rage. Destruction.

I was afraid to give into those emotions. To add fuel to her fire. Instead, I searched for the angel mojo.

And couldn't find it.

Wings. *Where are my wings?*

Struggling, I floundered again, my energy crackling from the fire. Nothing would be left.

"Bring her to the light," I heard a voice say.

Ragriel?

A blue spark. Fluttering wings. A melody that slipped through the fires.

There it was, the light. I feasted on it, cried for it.

Cool, feathery, cosmic. I dragged it in and flooded my system with it. The flames banked, the anger subsided.

I dumped it on Trinity with a laugh of satisfaction when she sucked in a surprised breath. The flood of watery magic knocked her off her magical feet. I felt her fall, gurgle, as if drowning.

Then I was being hauled out of her and back into my own body. I sputtered and opened my eyes to see Death and Ragriel peering down at me.

Death gave me a bored look. "Goofing off on the job again, I see. I repaired the rip in the veil. You can thank me later."

I coughed and told him what to do to himself in Romanian.

He grinned cheekily and gave a mock salute. "We could use your help here, you know."

I accepted his and Rag's outstretched hands and they hauled me to my feet. "Ragriel, you're still in angel form."

He nodded, pride lighting his features. "I *am* an angel."

Death slapped him on the back. "You need to rein in your sister, mate."

Another nod, this one serious. Trinity lay choking and spitting on the ground, her body spasming. "Is there any hope for her?" he asked.

My heart broke for him in that moment. "You can try."

"You bloody well cannot," Death countered. "Chloe, harvest her!"

"I did it...for you..." Trinity stretched out a hand to her brother. "I wanted to save you."

"I wish I could believe that," he replied.

Andy was retrieving Aurora's body from the rubble. Killion strode toward us, his clothes shredded, blood oozing from dozens of wounds. His face was contorted in bloodlust from the battle, but his eyes filled with relief at seeing me.

"I wanted you...to find...home," Trinity insisted, water running from her mouth with every word. "I swear."

I believed her. She'd lost her way, become the evil that so many had believed she was. It didn't excuse her actions, but made me understand how crucial it was to remember the fundamental adage that we all had good and evil inside us. It was what we chose to do with it that mattered.

Ghost returned. Corvus cried out a hello.

Andy shouted my name, weeping over Aurora's unmoving form. "Help her!"

The last of the demons were being hunted by those left standing. The place was a disaster, covered with body parts, blood, green goo, and worse. Fighting through the agony of broken ribs and smashed organs which were already mending themselves together, I retrieved my scythe from the monster's eye, then allowed Killion to guide me over to Trinity.

My ears rang and my skull hammered. "Time for you to go," I told her through gritted teeth.

"No!" She raised a hand to ward off the blade.

"I'll do it," Ragriel said, reaching for her.

"No." Mei Han appeared, a magical barrier snapping into place between him and Trinity. Several SMG employees in their black suits stood behind her. "The reaper harvests her and we take it from there."

"She doesn't technically have a soul," I told Mei. "At least none I can find."

"Neither of them do," Death said, jutting his chin at the siblings. "But he has something close to it."

"I'm aware." Mei glanced at me. "Harvest her. Now."

I wanted to demand an explanation, but Death caught my eye and shook his head. Fine with me. I could barely see straight and wanted to get as far from all of this as possible. "I'm sorry," I said to Ragriel. "Some rules are made to be followed."

Touching her with the death blade wasn't enough.

With the last of the dying demons shrieking around us and adding to my headache, I swung the scythe. "Trinity, you've been reaped."

Her demonic essence left, flickering and insubstantial, and I collapsed to the ground. Mei and her team took the wraith and her angel brother onto whatever awaited them on the other side. Killion and Death descended on me, trying to assess my wounds and offer help.

I still couldn't take an easy breath. "I'm fine," I lied. My body would be; my mind, I wasn't so sure about.

"Chloe!"

Andy's voice brought me out of my stupor. "Coming," I shouted.

Dread walked up my spine as Killion assisted me over to him. "She's dead," Andy cried, tears running down his cheeks. "She did this for *you*. Bring her back!"

"Aurora did this for *all* of us," Killion corrected. His hand settled on my low back. "She knew the risks."

I closed my eyes and searched for her spirit; found nothing. Had she already crossed?

I knelt beside her and touched her arm. In death, she was losing my looks and regaining her own.

"Give her your blood," Andy demanded of Killion. "Change her, now, before it's too late."

"I will not. She would be madder and more vengeful than these demons if I were to do so."

"He's right," I said. "She would hate being a vampire and each of us for forcing her into one."

Fierce animosity glowed in the shifter's eyes. The wolf paw tattoo on his neck pulsed. "*I can't lose her.*"

Tears filled my eyes. I wanted to raise her, but her

spirit was gone, and I would bring the wrath of Death down on me and Killion if I did so. I'd taken an oath not to be *that* grim—the one who defied my boss when it came to saving people I loved. Killion's Undead life was at stake--literally. "I'm so sorry."

He grabbed my arms and shook me. "Bring her back!"

Killion snarled and shoved Andy away. The shifter leaped up, prepared to lunge at him. "Stop!" I raised a hand. Closing my eyes, I reached for her soul again. I couldn't feel it. Either I was too exhausted, or something inside me was broken. I dropped my arm. "I'm sorry, Andy. I would if I could, but..."

Death appeared, surveying the ghouls feasting on the flesh and gooey blood of demons scattered across the nave. "That's the best you got, Grave Girl?"

I glanced up, wondering what he was getting at. "You said no more deals for saving people. Besides, I can't find her spirit."

"I did say that." He kicked at a severed limb. "But I've been known to change my mind."

I stood, wobbly, the world seeming to pulse along with my head. "Bring her back and take some of my years away."

"Chloe," Killion growled in warning.

I grabbed his hand and squeezed. "You would do the same if you were in my shoes." To Death, "I saved Yonah's soul. The least you can do is throw me a bone here."

The master vampire gave me a hard look, pressing his lips together to hold in his argument. He knew me better than anyone, and there was no talking me out of this. Instead, he addressed my boss. "After what the reaper has accomplished with all of our help, including the witch's, I think you owe it to her and the rest of us to simply extend Aurora's life. No consequences, no deals. Think of it as a gift. Something a *friend* would do."

Death tapped a finger against his chin as if thinking it over. "In this case, I prefer *favor* over gift." He smiled, all charm and deviousness. "You'll owe me a favor for this. Agreed?"

An immortal Fae king had taught me a lot about bargains. He and his kind were experts when it came to making them. "I agree to owe you one favor that doesn't involve or hurt anybody I care about during the dates of my SMG employment agreement and *only* if it is agreeable to me at the time of your request."

His magic swirled around me, teasing, taunting. "If you want the witch to live, this isn't a negotiation. Yes or no?"

Pepper and her sister joined us, Pepper placing a hand on Andy's shoulder as he dropped to his knees and pleaded with me. "Chloe, please."

I was too emotionally and mentally exhausted to try and outfox Death. Aurora's life was on the line. "Fine. I owe you a favor. Bring her back and—"

Aurora sat up and blinked. The sisters gasped and Andy let out a *whoop* as she asked, "Bring who back?"

Death made an exasperated sound and balled his hands into fists. "You had to go and ruin it, didn't you? Another two seconds was all I needed."

She glanced around at our happy faces. Her fingers

wiped the wetness from Andy's cheeks as she said to me, "Thanks for the mojo."

Death turned on me and I frantically shook my head. "I didn't do anything, I swear."

She cut her gaze between us, understanding hitting home. "Of course not," she backtracked, rubbing her head and wiping blood from her top lip. She stood with Andy's help. "I'm a necromancer. If I can't bring myself back, I'm not a very good one, am I?"

We all laughed, except for Death, who'd finally been outmaneuvered for real.

"Get some rest," he said to me in a petulant tone as he strode for the exit filled with rubble. "You've got recruits to train before you leave for Romania." He disappeared into the night.

Romania. My wedding. I shot a wobbly smile at Killion and he returned it.

"And our grandmother?" Pepper asked. "Is she...?"

Ghost came in for a pet, her giant head knocking into me and nearly sending me tumbling. Killion kept me balanced and I stroked between her ears. "She's in the afterlife, safe and sound. Said to tell you how much she loves you both."

The sisters held each other and wept bittersweet tears.

"This puts a damper on the party," Katarina said, wiping green goo off her thigh. "Maybe we should reschedule."

Andy was hanging onto Aurora, whispering things in her ear and making her giggle. He broke off and glanced at the destruction. He held up five fingers and shifters snapped to attention. "Cleanup crew. Get started." As they immediately began, he addressed us. "Together, we can get this place back to normal by Friday night. What do you think, Killion?"

The master vampire sent mental messages to several of his nest, and they joined Andy's crew. "I believe you are correct."

Andy extended a hand and the two males shook. Andy turned to Katarina. "I'm going to take Aurora home, but then I'll be back."

Aurora huffed. "Don't kid yourself. If the party is happening, you need my magic to assist in restoring this place." She made a face at the grotesque scene, the ghouls snacking away. "I'm not going anywhere."

Farina and Pepper broke apart, and Farina said, "We're holding a ceremony for Grandmother tomorrow night. You're all invited."

"We'd be honored," Andy replied.

My legs shook. "Can you handle the cleanup without me?" I asked Katarina. "I need to get rid of my headache and recharge my batteries before I'm going to be any good to you."

For once, the vampire placed a gentle hand on my shoulder. "You've done enough for tonight. We'll handle it from here. I expect you to be front and center Friday evening, though."

"You got it." I just then remembered that Killion and I had missed Nita's party. I would have a lot of apologizing to do—what was new? Somehow I'd have to make it up to her. "You can stay," I told Killion. "I'll call Rafael for a ride."

"The others will handle it." He retrieved the scythe's sheath and placed the weapon inside it. "Let's get you home."

Home—we were all searching for it and only finding it in each other. I leaned on Killion and he led me away.

We'd only gone a few feet when the ghoul queen appeared, blocking our path. "You survived," she purred at Killion. She seemed surprised, and a touch disappointed.

I snarled, some primitive part of me wanting to rip her head off. "Take your ghouls and go back where you came from. If I ever see you or them in this territory again, I'll make sure it's the last time you step foot here."

"Irascible as always." She glided closer, focusing on my mate. "No appreciation for what I did, Lord Reveux? Where is my daughter?"

He tightened his grip on me, pinning my hands at my sides before I could go for her neck. "You played the fence. Only when you saw the tide turn in our favor did you aide us."

Her nose flared. "A good leader keeps herself, as well as those in her charge, as safe as possible, but you overcame your enemies because we sided with you. Give me what belongs to me."

He heaved a tired sigh, even as his vampires drew around us, a force, an army, to be reckoned with. "Release," he said.

An invisible door in the giant statue of St. Anne at the front of the nave opened. One of Killion's vampire guards stepped out with a bound female in tow.

"Badhi," Aveena said on a sharp exhale.

The bindings disappeared and the hybrid ran to her mother. Aveena sneered at Killion as she wrapped her in a hug. "Buried her, did you?"

There was something in his eyes, his aura, when he replied. "If you ever defy me or my nest again, or bring any harm to our territory, she will be fair game and indeed see the inside of a coffin. You've been warned." He raised his voice. "Leave now. All of you. Or I'll have you removed."

Aveena narrowed her eyes. "I'll remember this. How you treated us." She snapped her fingers as she turned to go, an arm around Badhi. Her family fell into a line, ducklings following their mother. I covered my nose. "We'll be seeing you again, Lord Reveux."

Those of us left behind stayed still and silent, watching them. I felt their slimy magic receding, my own curling around me and Killion. Even with her gone, I felt like I needed a shower to wash away the ick factor, but there was a part of me that was relieved Killion had not buried the hybrid alive.

Outside, Moss drove into the parking lot. My legs gave out at the sight of the carnage to the church and graveyard. Ghost, back to her normal size, snorted with seeming disgust at my feet. Corvus flew overhead, his croak sad. "Wait. Where's Mason and Harlow?"

"Mason was injured. She took him home to mend."

I sagged. "Will he be all right?"

"He'll be fine. It was a challenge for him to fight side-by-side with shifters, but he overcame his prejudices and did well tonight."

The teen had been attacked by a group of shifters a

few months back, so his bias was warranted. "Why did Harlow let him come? He's a kid. It was too risky," I rambled on, my thoughts coming and going faster than I could catch up with them. "He could've been killed."

"But he wasn't. This was as much his fight, his future, as it was the rest of us. He wanted to be a part of it, and his mother agreed he should."

Pennyworth hopped from the front seat. He held out a travel mug to me. "Drink. Immediately. You look like a ghost."

Coming back from the dead was never a joyride. After being possessed by Ragriel, it seemed even harder. My magic felt fragmented; my brain exploding with random ideas as if they were popcorn. If I could get rid of the killer headache caused by it, that would help.

I accepted the offering and Killion's guidance into the backseat. Ghost jumped up front with Moss and the butler, Corvus sailing away in the night sky.

After sucking down every drop of the milkshake in the travel cup, I was asleep on Killion's shoulder before we reached the penthouse.

TWENTY-THREE

Sleep was what I needed, yet once I was safe in the master vampire's bed, nightmares haunted me. Yonah, Trinity, the beast. Every time I drifted off, one of them took me on a terrifying journey through my memories. I was stuck inside Ragriel's head, or fighting the towering monster again, over and over. I was trying to save everyone, and had to watch all the people I cared about being cut down, torn apart, burnt to a crisp by hot flames. Eaten by ghouls.

I woke up screaming, and Killion would hold me, listening to my sobbing explanations about the horrible scenarios my subconscious spun out. Even awake and cradled in his arms, I would hear Trinity's voice, or find myself floating in the in-between worlds, unable to stay present in the physical one. The earthbound ghosts that roamed the city tugged at me. Bodies in graveyards whimpered and pleaded for my attention.

At least, it seemed that way. I had trouble separating reality from my mind's confusion.

I struggled to stop seeing the horrors I had lived through. Over and over again, I relived the worst moments of my life, including my parents' tragic deaths.

At one point, Pennyworth burst into the bedroom after my latest scream echoed through the penthouse. Killion snarled at him to get out, while he rocked me like a baby.

The butler set a tray on the bed, his worried eyes boring into mine. A whole chocolate fudge cake and three pints of ice cream surrounded it. "Dairy helps her sleep," he growled at Killion.

He turned on his heel and marched out, slamming the door behind him.

"He only wants to help," I said through gritted teeth, reaching for a spoon. As usual, I was starving and food was always a panacea.

Killion took the utensil from my shaking fingers and began feeding me a bite of cake, followed by one of ice cream. "We all wish to ease your mind. What was this one about?"

I related what I could remember, shivering with a cold that would not leave my bones, regardless of the layers of blankets and the fire in the hearth. "Something's not right." I tapped my temple. "Up here."

"Not surprising." He fed me more. "You were possessed, drugged by an angel, and you died and came back. Again."

How many times did that make now? I'd lost count. Aurora kept telling me that I was a cat, but I did have a limit to how many times my body could go through the death experience and return intact. Right now, I wasn't worried about my physical body, but my mind was a mess. "I'll ask Aurora if she has a tea that can help."

"You must be desperate if you're willing to turn to such an extreme measure."

I sensed the teasing under his words and tried to smile. "I *am* desperate."

"Let me feed you."

He meant with his blood. I wasn't sure it would help, but I was indeed desperate. I swiped a bit of chocolate frosting onto my fingertip and held it to his lips. "Maybe you can distract me with something else as well."

He sucked the icing off and instantly we were ready to feed ourselves in a whole different manner. At least *that* was normal.

We spent the rest of that afternoon taking turns pleasuring each other, sleeping, and eating. Pennyworth was right—dairy did have a way of easing me into rest, as did being taken care of by my eternal soulmate. When I slept, I did so without dreams.

I wasn't fully online by eight, but I didn't want to miss the ceremony to honor Yonah. Against Killion's wishes, I forced him to take me to the private cemetery. Andy and Aurora were already there.

The gathering was small but the magic was powerful. Yonah's remains were re-buried in a fresh grave with a new spirit bag. Painted on it was an image of a hummingbird, as well as a coyote. As Pepper sang her favorite song, I felt the elder's spirit sweep around us, gently brushing over each of her family members.

When it was over, we were invited to the community hall for a party. I was already sagging, so I begged off, but asked if I could return when I was feeling better. I wanted to leave flowers at the site. The sisters expressed their appreciation and invited me to coffee the following week.

Although Killion had left word with Nita about me being sick and apologizing for missing her party, the coffee invitation gave me an idea. The next morning, I met my friend at The Smoking Bean and treated her to her favorite beverage and pastry.

"Don't think you're off the hook," she said around a mouthful of muffin. "Were you really sick?"

"Trust me," I told her. Every once in a while, I would simply lose track of time, or see things that weren't there. I continued to hear voices and felt itchy about all the dead nearby. A ghost in the corner of the shop kept trying to get my attention. "I was deathly ill and I'm still off."

She watched as I dug into my own muffin. "Looks like your appetite is fine."

I did have an iron stomach. "I'm grateful for that."

We shared a smile. She sipped her drink. "Is it the wedding? You've had quite a bit on your plate. A lot of anxiety. Could be messing with your game. Don't take this wrong, but maybe you need to make an appointment with Dr. Maxwell."

The grief counselor had released me from care during the summer, stating I was as sound and normal as I would ever be. She'd left the door open in case I had any setbacks, but I'd been happy to leave therapy behind. "I'll be all right. I just need time."

"I can fill in at the clinic for you."

She already had been. I was grateful that Harlow, too,

had pitched in on surgery day, even though Dr. O'Leary didn't like her. "I appreciate it. I think I need a few more days to recoup. Do something besides work and study."

"Speaking of, The Bridal Barn is having a big sale Friday and Saturday. If you're not up to it, no problem, but I thought I would mention it."

There was an invitation in her eyes I couldn't ignore. I finished my muffin. "I have a surprise for you."

She put down her coffee. "You found a dress."

"Sort of. I'm having one made."

"What?" She did a little dance in her seat. "Will it be ready in time?"

"My first fitting will be in a few weeks. I'd like you to go with me."

"Justin Timberlake couldn't stop me." She'd been in love with him since our teen years. "I can't wait to see it."

"I still need to find shoes and a veil."

"I thought you didn't want a veil."

Had I said that? I combed my memory but only came up with more horrors from the past few days and quickly shut the door on that. "I haven't decided for sure."

"Bridal Barn has accessories *and* shoes." She swirled her cup and sipped. "I know a gal who works there. She can be our personal shopper for an hour Friday, if you're game."

Shopping. Hanging out with my bestie. Maybe I'd feel normal, at least for those sixty minutes. "Throw in lunch and I'm in."

She smacked the table. "You got it."

"We'll find your maid of honor dress, too."

Her grin grew. "This is going to be fun."

I sure hoped so. She had to go to work and we promised to text later.

Moss waited for me outside, but I told him I wanted to walk for a bit. I strolled, breathing in the fall air, and then swung by the clinic. Patty had Corvus and Ghost "helping" her, and they both greeted me in their own ways.

"Feeling better?" she asked.

I tucked Ghost under my arm and petted one of the raven's wings. He was on his perch and said "kill" about twenty times. Patty hadn't had much luck teaching him new words. "Some. This virus is nasty and even though I'm not contagious anymore, I'm feeling the burn."

"We sure have missed you, but you take as much time as you need. We're not going anywhere." She tidied a stack of folders on her desk. "I apologize for getting so upset the other day. I know you're doing your best."

"Thanks, Patty. I really am." I signed a few checks for her, then hooked Ghost to her leash and took her with me. Killion would pick up Corvus later.

I was by the park near my apartment building when I saw Vera walking with Frank. Each of them had a dog, and they were laughing and having a good time. I started to join them, then decided it was better to leave them be. I'd tease her later, sure my matchmaking skills had achieved their goal.

The fresh air and normal noises of humans going about their lives restored some of my sanity. Instead of demon voices, I tuned into birdsong. Rather than feeling like I was sinking into a pit of green goo, I noticed the grass, stubbornly clinging to life even though we'd had a lot of chilly nights. The clay soil shimmered in the sun and most folks who'd put out Halloween decorations had not taken them down yet. I had to avoid looking at the skeletons and jack-o'-lanterns, but I enjoyed the mums and fall leaves.

Death appeared in my path on my way back downtown. He had an older guy with piercings and eye makeup in tow. "Meet your new trainee," Death said, patting the tall, angular guy on the back. "This is Diego Benson."

I froze. "Ragriel?"

"Shh." He looked around as if someone might overhear, then announced loudly, "Friends call me Die. I know Diego is pronounced *dee*-a-go, but I like how Die sounds. Tough and dangerous, you know."

"Don't ask questions," Death said to me. "Just go with it." Then he disappeared.

"Great," I murmured. Ghost barked a hello.

Ragriel—Diego—knelt and held out a hand to let her sniff. "I don't think we've officially met. What's your name, little doggie?"

"Ghost," I told him. "I assume Mei doesn't know you're here?"

He slid his eyes around again and motioned at me to lower my voice. "I feel I have a debt to pay and Death suggested this was a way to do it. You have to pretend you don't know me, though, okay?" The look he gave me oozed sincerity. "I appreciate everything you did for me."

I swallowed the lump in my throat. My good mood evaporated, the memories still too fresh. "You do anything out of line and I will make you wish you hadn't come back."

He crossed a finger over his heart. "Best behavior. This is a fresh start for me. I have my own body! Pretty cool, huh?" Ghost licked his fingers and he laughed. "She's awesome. This world is awesome." His arms went wide as he stood, and I thought he was going to hug me. "You're awesome!"

Taking a step out of reach, I sighed. "I gather you haven't gotten your psychopomp yet?"

Disappointed I didn't embrace him, he dropped his arms and shook his head. "It's my first day. I hope I get a dog like her."

"Do you have your grim manual?"

His face brightened. "Yeah, some guy named Tinder gave it to me." He held up a thumb, eyeballing the end. "Do they always make you sign in blood?"

I had so much to tell him, show him. "Did you volunteer or did Death force you into this?"

"Oh, no, I volunteered. I..." He appeared abashed. "I really like you."

Reaper's keepers. "Don't even go there. I'm glad things are working out for you, but we are not friends. Got it?"

His smile didn't dim one bit. "Can I have your autograph?"

"No, and don't look at me that way." Where to start with his training? "Do you drink coffee?"

"The elixir of life? You know it."

Okay, at least that was common ground. "Your assignment today is to go to The Smoking Bean and order your favorite drink. Tell the gal working, Nita, that it's on me. She makes the best lattes, so get one of those. She doesn't know we're grims, or anything about the magical world, so keep the woo-woo talk to yourself, okay?"

"Um, sure. Then what?"

"Try on your robes, check out your new grim tattoo, and wait for your psychopomp to show up."

"That's it?"

"Training officially starts Monday." Maybe by then, I'd be back to normal and have a plan to deal with him. "Do you have a place to stay?"

"I do." He sounded thrilled about it. "There's this hotel called the Beaumont a few blocks from here and Death got me a room. It's really nice."

For a moment, I couldn't respond. "That Death," I ground out. "He's something, isn't he?"

A nod. "Says he's your biggest fan, but I think I can give him a run for his money on that."

Yeah. Okay, then. "How about a phone? Did he give you one of those?"

He fished in his back pocket and held out a brand new, top of the line one that matched mine. "I'm not great with technology, but I'm learning."

I took it from him and opened his contacts. "I'll put my number in here. If anything weird happens between now and then, check your manual first, then give me a call."

"Hey," a voice said. "I thought I made the best lattes." Mason came around the corner, grinning. He looked like his normal self and I was relieved. "Mom said you could use help at the clinic. Is it okay if I pitch in?"

"Are you sure you're up for it?"

"Grave Girl, jeez. I'm totally fine. Hi, I'm Mason." He held out a hand to Diego. "I'm not mundane, so feel free to ask me questions about the supernatural. You coming to the party Friday night?"

"There's a grim party?"

Mason curled his top lip back, revealing a fang. "It's all inclusive, man. The more the merrier."

I handed the cell back to Diego. "We're working on community rapport. You're welcome to come." I would probably regret that.

His grin could have lit the entire block. "Awesome. I'll clear my calendar. Which way is the coffee shop?"

We both pointed and he headed off to The Bean. Mason elbowed me. "I heard you were upset about me participating in the fight."

I pulled him to me and gave him a fierce hug. "I thought we'd lost you."

"You seriously underestimate me," he said, disengaging himself from my grip. He walked backwards so he faced me as I strolled down the sidewalk. "You were just worried about me not being around to make your favorite drink."

"Busted. Are you heading to the clinic?"

"Nah, Megan's in school for another hour, and I'm only really doing this so I can hang out with her. Killion signed me up for an online business class and he'll bust my fangs if I don't get my lesson done. Catch you later."

He was a mini-Killion in the making. "You'll be taking over the world in no time."

"World domination is so yesterday. I'm taking over the universe."

I laughed as he disappeared.

I napped that afternoon, sleeping soundly. I felt more like myself when I woke.

Killion was on the veranda, hands gripping the railing, his jaw set as he stared at the downtown area. I sensed he wasn't actually seeing the cars and folks going by.

I slid my arms around his waist and rested my head on his back. "Are you worried about Friday night?"

His tense muscles relaxed. "Not that." He turned in my arms to look at me. "How are you feeling?"

"Immensely better. My brain seems to require more time to heal than my body."

He brushed hair from my cheek, the afternoon sun already losing its warmth to the twilight creeping across the town. "I wish there were more I could do."

"There's not, so stop beating yourself up."

He rubbed my arms as I rested my head on his chest. "I thought Aveena would be true to her word, especially with the threat to her daughter. I should have used compulsion on her. I was trying to be more like you, allow her free will, but it nearly cost us everything."

His inability to chase away my demons wasn't the only thing bugging him. He couldn't stop his Monday-morning quarterbacking. "In case you didn't notice, we won. The only thing she and her ghouls were good for was cleanup. We didn't need her."

He stroked my back, sending warm tingles over me. "It was poor strategy on my part. I should have compelled her, and Aurora should have used some type of spell to keep Trinity from astral projecting. The shifters need more training."

"Are you kidding me right now? That was the most amazing battle I've ever witnessed, and along with our friends' abilities, we never would have won if it weren't for your brilliant tactics."

We stayed that way for a long few minutes, and I knew he was still unhappy with himself, but there wasn't much I could do to change his mind. Distraction was my only option.

I drew away and slipped a strap of my nightgown down my arm, then the other, giving him a coy look as I held the garment in place over my breasts. "Perhaps you'd like to teach me more strategy in the bedroom."

He stilled, that preternatural posture and the accompanying crook of his mouth sending shivers down my spine that had nothing to do with the approaching night. "A good soldier knows how to take commands."

I let the nightgown fall to pool at my feet, then sashayed into the bedroom. "I promise to be nothing but a good soldier." And then I squealed when he caught me up and dumped me on the mattress.

TWENTY-FOUR

Friday afternoon, Nita and I had a blast looking at dresses and accessories. I left The Bridal Barn with shoes and stockings. No veil; I decided against it since it was yet another thing that reminded me of Trinity. Nita found plenty of options for her own wedding dress, but not a maid of honor one for my ceremony. I had an idea and contacted Estrid, who begrudgingly told me to bring her by and she would design something for her.

My mind had become more centered and less distracted by random thoughts and memories. I still experienced an occasional nightmare, but I chalked it up to post traumatic stress and didn't worry about it. I had too many other things going on.

That night, the party was in full swing by the time Killion and I arrived. I made him stop first at the cemetery so I could tell Dottie Mae that Curtis had died thirty years ago and was already on the other side from my research. She'd been angry about that, but after that, she'd willingly gone to the afterlife for me, probably ready to find him over there and give him an earful.

Katarina, dressed in a slinky black number, greeted us with cups of blood.

Yummy.

I handed mine to Killion and went to say hi to Andy and Aurora. I checked in with Pepper and Farina, nodded at Harlow, and thumbs upped Mason, who had brought Megan. She was mundane, but knew about vampires and this world, and if his mother had okayed it, then I had to get on board.

The church had been repaired and looked exactly the way it had before. Every once in a while, I caught movement out of the corner of my eye that made me freeze, a knee-jerk reaction. With all of the swirling magics in the place, I felt a little twitchy.

I gritted my teeth, forced myself to smile, and pretended I was having a good time. This was of utter importance to everyone involved, especially Killion. He needed this to go well.

Diego arrived and hailed me, crossing the room under Killion's watchful eye. I'd told him about Ragriel becoming a new man, thanks to Death, and that he was my first trainee. The master vampire wasn't any happier about the situation than I was, but we'd agreed to give Die a chance. "That grim manual is something else, isn't it?" Diego asked, bopping slightly to the pulsating music the DJ was playing. "How do you remember all of the rules and regulations?"

I didn't, but it was best not to confess that tidbit. "I'll

make sure you learn the important ones. Any sign of your psychopomp?"

"About that." He reached inside his denim jacket and produced a guinea pig. "This is Hal. Hal—you know, short for Halloween?"

It had three equal bands across its body, two black and one white. I took the small rodent, holding it up to look in its eyes. "Hi, Hal. Nice to meet you. You look like an Oreo cookie."

The guinea pig rolled its head, shuddered once, and grew ten times its size, causing me to drop it. He landed on all four feet, snorted, and then sat back on his hind legs and started cleaning his face.

Shifters and vamps nearby gasped, backed away, and eyed us. The music screeched to a halt.

"He's having a bit of trouble controlling himself," Die announced. "We're working on it. Trust me, you don't want a guinea pig this size peeing in your house."

His chuckle only garnered odd looks from those gathered. I laughed and Killion motioned at the DJ. Music once again filled the air and the group returned to their dancing, drinking, and talking. "We'll work on that next week, too," I told Die.

He patted the guinea pig, and it shuddered again, becoming hand-size once more. Just as it started to run, he grabbed it. Hal squeaked, and Die tucked it back inside his jacket. "I never had a pet growing up. Kind of hoped I'd finally get a dog, but I guess Hal is it."

"How did he come to you?"

"This gal, Vera. I guess she and her sister, Velma, pick up a lot of rescues and find homes for them. Anyway, I wanted a dog and mentioned it to that friend of yours, Nita, at the coffee shop. Vera was behind me and said I should go see her sister. Except when I got there and I was checking out the ones available for adoption, I kept hearing this screeching noise. Saw Hal in a cage, running on a wheel. I thought he was cute and I went to pet him while Velma grabbed the adoption forms. Next thing I know, he morphed into this giant rodent and peed on me. I screamed, he morphed back, and Velma came running. I had to make up a story to explain why my pant leg was wet, but I knew I wasn't getting a dog for a psychopomp. I was getting him." He gave a *what can you* do shrug.

"My experience was similar. I'll tell you about it Monday."

The music stopped and Katarina's voice rang out. "Can I have your attention?" She stood on the dais, glancing over the crowd. "As all of you know, we might not be here tonight if it weren't for two very special indi-viduals."

Killion slid up next to me, his fingers entwining with mine. "What is she doing?" I asked under my breath.

The master vampire squeezed my hand. Out of the corner of my eye I saw he was smiling.

This couldn't be good.

Katarina raised her glass. "An alliance between the vampires and shifters strengthens all of us. We have Master Killion Reveux to thank for reaching out to the Shifter Nation and their leaders"—her glass swung to Andy and the other elders present—"for accepting that invitation."

A cheer went up and I relaxed, smiling as many

raised their drinks to Killion. I tried to step away, to give him the limelight, but he held onto me.

"We also have a reaper who stopped the demon witch from tearing our world apart," Katarina continued, "and who, I might add, makes the finest punching bag around."

The grin she gave me promised plenty more opportunities for me to be said bag. As applause broke out, along with a few errant whistles from Mason, I felt myself blush. She waved for Killion and I to join her, but I shook my head.

Killion tugged me into step with him. Along the way, Pepper and Farina reached out to touch my arms. Harlow patted my shoulder. The gathering fell quiet, all eyes on me as I stood flanked by the two vampires.

Diego, at the rear, waved. "I know her!" No one paid attention to him, but he kept nodding and grinning. "She's my mentor!"

"For those who *don't* know her," Killion announced, "this is Chloe Frost. While she is neither Undead, nor a shifter, she's my betrothed. She has earned my respect and that of my nest. Andy and I, along with many of you, have worked to bring this night to fruition, but we must also remember Chloe's part in restoring the veil between worlds."

"Actually," I interrupted, "that was Death."

Those gathered simply stared at me. Killion continued. "That veil *must* remain intact, or humanity will be destroyed and the supernatural community will end up slaves or worse to demons. It is imperative that we respect and appreciate the strengths of each other, and that we support this alliance. Together we can remain strong. Only united can we be the force demons fear."

A loud cry of conviction followed in unison, sending magic spiraling up and down my spine. I smiled, seeing the joy on the faces of those gathered. They believed in this alliance.

Andy and Aurora lifted their glasses high. Others joined in.

Hope for the future. Friendships between supernatural races.

Everything I'd been through had been worth it. Knowing Danté's Grove, and those I cared about, were safe gave me peace.

And a sense of pride.

I accepted a kiss from Killion in front of the crowd, fresh cheers and whistles accompanying my even more intense blush. Before we left the stage, Katarina chucked my chin. "Don't think I'm going easy on you just because you saved the world."

"I wouldn't dream of it." I made sure to pinch her in the side before Killion led me down the steps.

"I'll get you for that next week," she called.

I glanced over my shoulder and winked. "I look forward to it."

When we arrived home, Death waited in the foyer outside the penthouse door.

The master vampire unwound himself from me where he had me pressed against the elevator wall and sighed. "What do you want?"

"Chloe told me to come," Death said by way of explanation.

I squeezed Killion's arm. "The three of us need to talk." I strode for the door and waved at Death. "Come on in."

Pennyworth hovered as I got them seated at the dining room table. He brought Killion a glass of wine, a milkshake for me, and an espresso by request for Death. "What is this about?" Killion asked.

"Killion,"—I motioned from him to my boss—"meet your first client for Reveux Investigations." He arched a brow. "You don't like the name?"

His lips pursed. "We'll discuss that later." He shifted his attention to Death. "Well?"

Death fiddled with the tiny porcelain cup in his hands. "Chloe mentioned you might be willing to help me with a sensitive matter concerning SMG. It's..."

"Off the book," I supplied at his pause.

Death nodded. "They can't know."

Killion sipped his wine. "Investigating Mei?"

"Not specifically." Death sketched the details of what he'd been looking into regarding Ragriel and Trinity. "There could be more of these experiments. I've been following various leads but every time I'm close, the trail disappears. Whether there are more hybrids or not, I need to figure out who created the two we know about, and for what purpose. I don't know who I can trust, and if I get caught, the consequences will be dire."

From the look in Killion's eyes, I could see the wheels already turning. "You brought Ragriel back."

"He has a soul of some kind," I said. "Trinity, though, did not."

"If whoever created them is not on SMG's radar, why should it be on yours?" Killion asked.

Death eased back in his seat, setting down the cup and crossing his arms over his massive chest. "That's the thing, mate. It *should* be on their radar. I knew about Ragriel, but only peripherally when Grim Zero was tasked to take him out. At that time, there were other priorities on my plate. I didn't give it my full attention, but this round I did. He shouldn't have a soul. Trinity shouldn't have had a contract. They're not like the rest of us, and there's something messed up about how they came into existence. It definitely wasn't the normal way."

Killion drummed his fingers on the table, the wheels continuing to turn. "If there's no one higher up we can trust, how do you suggest we get answers?"

Death grinned. "You're the brains of this operation."

"And you are?" Killion asked.

"The muscle and magic. Duh."

Killion was quiet so long, I anticipated a "no." He surprised me when he said, "I'll draw up a contract, and we'll reconvene Monday to discuss our first move."

Death downed his drink and stood. "Could be dangerous, you know."

Killion fingered his glass, flicking his gaze to me from under his brows. "I rather enjoy danger."

Death held out his fist and Killion reluctantly bumped it. "To new ventures," Death said. "And to friendship."

That night in bed, Killion opened his philosophy book and began reading to me. I snuggled close and let his voice soothe me. In the last sentence, the philosopher said, "*We are only as strong as the love we give. Only find our true place in the world through those we give it to.*"

Killion closed the book and kissed me, and for once, I enjoyed the philosopher's take on life. "I agree," I said. "Who is this guy, anyway?"

He stunned me when he said, "My father."

I rose on an elbow. "What?"

Staring at the slim volume, he nodded. "It's poetry as much as philosophy, this book. He wrote it for my mother."

True soulmates. "You didn't tell me that."

"Did you enjoy any of it?"

I would have enjoyed it more if I'd known his father had wrote it for her. "He was incredibly smart, like you, wasn't he? He must have loved her very much."

"He did." The corner of his mouth twitched in a smile as memories surfaced, then faded away. "He was a hard, brutal vampire. Spared no quarter for those who hunted us. But when it came to her, he was absolutely lost."

"I prefer smitten." At his glance, I dropped a kiss on his lips. "Just like you are with me."

"You are mine and I am yours," he said against my mouth. "You are home for me."

"And you me."

He deepened the kiss and was lifting the edge of my sleep shirt when we broke apart. "No matter where we go, or what happens in this world, we have each other."

"In this world and the next," I said. It was one of our oaths as *incatusa sufletum*.

He stared into my eyes, my soul. "In this world and the next."

I fell asleep in his arms later that night and dreamed of castles in Romania.

CHLOE AND KILLION *are happy for now, but don't miss what happens when they head for Killion's true home for their wedding in the next exciting installment,* Grim Vows, *coming 2024.*

Paranormal Urban Fantasy:

The Accidental Reaper Paranormal Urban Fantasy Series Special Collection

Killin' It (short story for newsletter subscribers only)

The Vampire's Kiss (an exclusive short story available ONLY in Misty's Store. *Intended for mature audiences 17+)*

Grave Girl

Kali Sweet Urban Fantasy Series Books 1-3

Sweet Curse, Kali Sweet Urban Fantasy Series, Book 4

Paranormal Contemporary Romance:

Witches Anonymous Step 1

Jingle Hells, WA Step 2

Wicked Souls, WA Step 3

Dark Moon Lilith, Witches Anonymous Step 4

Dancing With the Devil, Witches Anonymous Step 5

Devil's Due, Witches Anonymous Step 6

Dirty Deeds, Witches Anonymous Step 7

Wicked Wedding, Witches Anonymous Step 8

Paranormal Romantic Suspense:

Soul Survivor, Moon Water Series, Book 1

Soul Protector, Moon Water Series, Book 2

Cozy Mysteries (writing as Nyx Halliwell):

Sister Witches Of Raven Falls Mystery Series

Sister Witches of Raven Falls Special Collection

Of Potions and Portents

Of Curses and Charms

Of Stars and Spells

Of Spirits and Superstition

Confessions of a Closet Medium Cozy Mystery Series

Confessions of a Closet Medium Special Collection

Pumpkins & Poltergeists

Magic & Mistletoe

Hearts & Haunts

Vows & Vengeance

Cupcakes & Corpses

Tea Leaves & Troubled Spirits

Sister Witches of Story Cove (Formerly Once Upon a Witch) Cozy Mystery Series

Cinder

Belle

Snow

Ruby

Zelle

Don't want to miss a single release? Sign up for my newsletter today! http://eepurl.com/bP19Lr

Are you caught up with my books?

https://mistyevansbooks.com/book-list-2

SEALs of Shadow Force Romantic Suspense Series Box Set, Books 1-7

SEALS of Shadow Force Series: Spy Division

Man Hunt

Man Killer

Man Down

Covert Affairs

Covert Tactics

Covert Obsession (2024)

SCVC Taskforce Set Books 1-10

SCVC Taskforce Romantic Suspense Series Books

Super Agent Romantic Suspense Series Books 1-7

The Justice Team Series (with Adrienne Giordano)

Stealing Justice

Cheating Justice

Holiday Justice

Exposing Justice

Undercover Justice

Protecting Justice

Missing Justice

Defending Justice

SCHOCK SISTERS MYSTERY SERIES
w/Adrienne Giordano

1st Shock

2nd Strike

3rd Tango

The Secret Ingredient Culinary Mystery Series

The Secret Ingredient, A Culinary Romantic Mystery with Bonus Recipes

The Secret Life of Cranberry Sauce, A Secret Ingredient Holiday Novella

MEET MISTY

USA TODAY Bestselling Author Misty Evans has published over eighty fiction novels, as well as nonfiction inspirational journals. She loves writing romantic suspense, urban fantasy, and paranormal romance. Under her pen name, Nyx Halliwell, she also writes paranormal mysteries.

When not reading or writing, she enjoys music, movies, and hanging out with her husband, twin sons, and three spoiled rescue dogs. She's a crafter at heart and has far too many projects to finish.

Don't want to miss a single adventure? Visit www.mistyevansbooks.com to become a VIP and find out ALL the news!

Hello Beautiful Reader!

Thank you for reading this story! It is an honor and a privilege to write books for you. I'm an indie author and every fan is important to me. I pour my heart into each story and do my best to bring you an escape from the real world.

I hope you enjoyed this one, and if so, would you mind leaving a review at your favorite retailer? Or share your enjoyment of it with a friend or family member? I'd really appreciate it, and reviews help other readers find books they will love, too.

Readers are the key to my success - not a traditional publishing deal (had four), an agent (had two), or a publicity team (yep, you guessed it, had several of those as well.)

Those of you who read my books and love my characters and worlds, and who then tell others are like the best of friends. I adore you and will keep writing if you keep reading!

If you'd like to learn about my other books, sales, and special promotions, please sign up for my newsletter at **www.mistyevansbooks.com**. You'll get coupons to download starter packs for FREE, whether you love my romantic suspense or my paranormal. I also have a spy quiz, and a book list you can download and print.

Support me directly (no retailer taking their cut), grab special edition box sets, and get new releases before they are out at retailers by visiting my store **https://mistye vansbooks.com/shop**. I have sales and offer NEW RELEASES early! Check it out.

Last but not least, if you enjoy clean, cozy mysteries, visit my pen name **www.nyxhalliwell.com** to see those books.

Thank you and happy reading!
Misty